BRIE'S SUBMISSION

Her Russian Returns

Passion and pain

Red Phoenix

Red Phoenix

Print Edition
www.redphoenixauthor.com

Her Russian Returns: Brie's Submission
15th of the Brie Series

Edited by Jennifer Blackwell and Karen Koehler
Proofed by Becki Wyer & Marilyn Cooper
Cover by Shanoff Designs
Formatted by BB eBooks
Phoenix symbol by Nicole Delfs

Dedication

I want to thank MrRed, who continues to be so supportive of my work.

It's not just the inspiration he provides, but the care and patience

he gives me as a writer.

He understands when I laugh or cry for no apparent reason

as scenes from the story play out in my head at random moments.

LOL

I also want to give special thanks to my children.

Their enthusiastic support of my work has been a blessing and a joy.

To my cast of fans who work diligently behind the scenes, my deepest thanks.

Your hard work and belief in me never ceases to amaze and inspire.

To every person who has taken the time to write an email, seek me out on social media, go to an author event, or send me a gift or a letter.

You blow me away!

I am every bit your fan, as you are mine. ~Red

YOU CAN ALSO BUY THE AUDIO BOOK!

Her Russian Returns #15

Narrated by Aiden Snow

SIGN UP FOR MY NEWSLETTER HERE FOR THE LATEST RED PHOENIX UPDATES

FOLLOW ME ON INSTAGRAM

INSTAGRAM.COM/REDPHOENIXAUTHOR

SALES, GIVEAWAYS, NEW RELEASES, PREORDER LINKS, AND MORE!

SIGN UP HERE

REDPHOENIXAUTHOR.COM/NEWSLETTER-SIGNUP

CONTENTS

Shocking Truths....1

Guardian Angel....15

Mamulya....34

Freedom....45

The Sacrifice....60

Lesson in Sadism....75

Her Voice....87

Vodka Shot....97

Reconciliation....109

Payback....125

Heaven....138

Unity....152

Home....165

Making Amends....184

Legacy....203

Big Guns....217

The Chase....227

Mos-*cow*....246

Coming Next....260

About the Author....261

Other Red Phoenix Books....264

Connect with Red on Substance B....269

Shocking Truths

Rytsar's return to consciousness was a painful one. His head throbbed like a jackhammer was driving into his skull, the pain so intense it made him nauseous.

Taking a survey of his surroundings without opening his eyes, Rytsar noted first the engine roar of a small airplane. He could only guess where they were taking him—he had expected to be dead by now.

Resisting the urge to retch, Rytsar lay perfectly still, his survival instincts alerting him to the fact he was being watched as he lay there. With difficulty, he kept his breath even as an intense pain shot through his abdomen, making him want to scream in agony.

Eventually, someone stood up and walked over to him, giving Rytsar a kick in the stomach. It took everything in him not to react, but when he didn't respond, the man complained.

"The fucking coward is still out. All this waiting is annoying me." He must have swung back his leg for another kick because the commanding voice of their leader rang out.

"*Nyet*! Durov is now the property of the Koslovs. You hurt him again and it will cost you your life."

"But he insulted the brothers in front of us. Surely that deserves punishment."

"It is the only reason I did not kill you when you pummeled him in the hospital. The brothers were very clear about the condition of this package we're delivering."

"But what about Orlov? He almost killed the *mu'dak*."

The leader let out an amused snort in answer, letting Rytsar know the fate of the man who had tried to choke him to death. To defy a direct order from the Koslov brothers meant immediate death by the hands of their own.

Rytsar was not surprised, however; Orlov had never been particularly bright. He'd set his sights on Rytsar early on to prove to the *bratva* organization that he was a man to be reckoned with. Being the gnat that he was, he'd only made a pathetic nuisance of himself.

That is…until yesterday.

It seemed fitting that the idiot had been thwarted by a cat.

Rytsar had to keep his smile from his face, grateful he'd instructed Titov to set up a monthly shipment of caviar and catnip be sent to Thane's home. It was a fair repayment for his debt, and might help convince his comrade to keep the animal.

While he'd never become a pet lover, Rytsar definitely had feelings for that black tom cat and hoped Thane would reconsider his own stance on housing pets.

Rytsar's thoughts were interrupted when he heard one of them ask, "What happens if he doesn't wake up?"

"We're all dead," the leader said without hesitation.

Rytsar was violently shaken by the man who had kicked him, which he now thought of as the instigator. "Wake up, you fucking *mu'dak*. I'm not dying because of you."

Suddenly a scuffle broke out as the man was taken to the ground. "You touch him again, and I will kill you with my bare hands," the leader growled ominously.

Rytsar found it amusing that even lying there bound and defenseless, he still wielded power over all these men.

The landing hours later was rough and bumpy, which alerted Rytsar to his location. He knew that the Koslov brothers had a secret place somewhere up in the north. The jarring landing indicated it was a makeshift runway, and Rytsar suspected their location was somewhere in the middle of the frozen Siberian forest.

Such an isolated place allowed them to do whatever they wished without the risk of detection, and the Koslov brothers were notorious for their ability to make people disappear without a trace.

Rytsar had always assumed their influence was limited only to Russia, but after what had just happened in America, he understood they were now a global threat. It made them exceedingly dangerous—as the two brothers were not stable.

Their lust for power and their impetuous nature made for a volatile and dangerous mixture.

Rytsar had recognized that early on when they were

still teenagers, and had avoided any dealings with the duo. Unfortunately, his father had not been so wise.

By all accounts, Rytsar should have been dead that day his mother was murdered and he'd stormed into the Koslovs' headquarters in full berserker mode. For some reason, he could remember nothing after charging into the room to find his father sitting at a card table, calmly making a bet.

Everything went red, all rational thought evaporating, as Rytsar gave in to the darkest part of his soul. He was told afterward that he'd put four of the Koslov men down and was about to attack another when the patriarch of their clan, Nikolay, ordered Rytsar be subdued and brought to his personal quarters.

It had been a great shock to wake up the next day—still alive. That hadn't been his plan when he'd tried to attack his father, and only meant he had to deal with the horrifying reality of his mother's death.

To make matters worse, it left him in the hands of his sworn enemy.

He did not know then that Nikolay was actually a friend.

"Finally back from the dead, I see," Nikolay stated in a low gravelly voice when Rytsar opened his eyes. The older gentleman was sitting across from him, seated in a large leather chair.

Rytsar bolted straight up to stand in a defensive

pose, the sudden movement causing an angry pounding in his head and chest.

"You are a bull when you lose your mind, Anton. It took eight of my men to finally take you down, and that was after you incapacitated five of them."

"Did I kill him?"

"Who? Your father?"

Rytsar said nothing, glaring at the man.

"Thankfully not, because I would not have been able to save you if you had. My grandsons are very possessive of your father for some unexplainable reason."

Rytsar snarled, knowing they were only using Vladimir as a pawn.

"Unfortunately," Nikolay continued, "my men paid the price protecting him from you."

"Why would you allow them to protect such a worthless coward as Vladimir Durov?" Rytsar spat.

Nikolay pressed his fingers together thoughtfully. "My grandsons have an unusual attachment to him that I do not care for, but after they publicly announced that he was under the protection of the Koslovs, I unwillingly became duty-bound to see he remains unharmed. To allow him to die would be a mark against our family. I cannot allow that as *Pakhan*."

"You should have let me kill him then! It would have been a win/win for the Koslov organization. You would have been rid of my worthless father and myself, with no one holding you responsible since his death was at the hands of his own son."

"I did not want to see you die."

Rytsar was surprised by his answer and instantly became suspicious. "Why? I am nothing to you."

Nikolay smiled amiably. "Did your grandfather ever speak of me?"

"On occasion. He said he respected you despite your connection to the *bratva*."

"He and I always had a mutual respect for each other, yes. What I admired in him, I see in you. It is the reason I ordered a stay of execution and had them bring you to my chambers."

"What? I am to become your prisoner waiting for my own death?"

Nikolay laughed, standing up. He was a giant of a man, towering over Rytsar. "No, Anton. You are not a prisoner here. You can leave right now if you wish. However, my grandsons want you dead and there will come a time when I will not be able to prevent it."

"Because?" Rytsar demanded.

Nikolay looked away and said in a resigned voice, "I will pass on to the other side and whether I want it or not, they will become the new ruling power."

"Those two are worthless. Unworthy of the Koslov name."

"I agree."

Rytsar's eyes narrowed. "Why would you say that? They are your kin."

"It's no different than you and your father. We do not choose our bloodline. Sometimes nature makes a mistake—in my case, two."

Rytsar snorted.

"Your grandfather found himself in the same predicament I find myself in now. But unlike me, who has no one else to choose from, he was able to pass over his son when it came time to grant his inheritance."

Rytsar frowned, growling in disgust. "This is nonsense! I have no idea what you are talking about."

"When your grandfather gave you his ring, he passed on everything he had to you."

"Hah! And why was I not made aware of this?" Rytsar scoffed sarcastically.

"Being a highly intelligent individual, your grandfather always had a method to his madness. Although your father knows exactly what that ring on your finger means, few others do. I suspect your grandfather wanted you to live out your youth unencumbered by the responsibility such wealth would bring."

Rytsar laughed ruefully. "Is *that* the reason you spared me? You want his money?"

"I have no interest in your inheritance," Nikolay replied, sounding insulted.

"I find it very odd that I was not made aware of this."

"You've been living off a portion of that inheritance since your grandfather died. Had you never questioned the source?"

"Naturally, I assumed it was funded by the inheritance but I was told the allowance came directly from my father."

"Sneaky *ublyudok*," Nikolay muttered under his breath.

"So are you trying to claim that all this time I have been rich but didn't know it?" Rytsar said with a dismissive laugh, certain he was being played but not comprehending why.

Nikolay answered in all seriousness, "There must be an age clause set in his will."

"Meaning?"

"The full inheritance will not be yours until a stipulated age. An age your grandfather deemed you would be old enough to properly control the power behind such wealth."

Rytsar narrowed his eyes. "If that is true, why would my father lead me to believe the inheritance had been passed down to him instead?"

"Such blatant deceit speaks to his hidden motive," Nikolay said in disgust. "I have long suspected Vladimir was up to no good."

"What are you saying?" Rytsar demanded.

"I firmly believe Vladimir hoped you would instigate your own demise. It's the only way the inheritance could end up in his hands."

The hairs stood up on the back of Rytsar's neck. "What exactly are you implying?"

"Your grandfather's inheritance would automatically revert to his only son should you commit suicide. If he could keep you ignorant of your wealth, it would give him significant leverage to begin stripping away your will to live."

A terrible thought flashed through Rytsar's mind as he contemplated what Nikolay was saying.

His grandfather had given him the ring a few months before he'd started courting Tatianna…

"It's not possible," Rytsar stated. The idea of it was too horrendous to voice aloud. He had held deep anger and resentment toward Titov for bringing the deadly taint of the *bratva* into Tatianna's life. But what if her kidnapping hadn't been Titov's fault?

Rytsar remembered well the day Titov came banging on his door, shouting that Tatianna was missing. They'd scoured Moscow until they found Yuri, the boy who had sold her off to protect his own life because of an unpaid gambling debt. They'd beaten the sniveling coward until he confessed his guilt and told them where she had been taken.

Rytsar had been only minutes away from rescuing her from the horrors that lay ahead, when she disappeared without a trace and the hunt to save her began.

He'd never seen that worm again or he would have killed the man with his bare hands for destroying Tatianna. At the time, Rytsar assumed he'd simply gone into hiding, knowing his life was forfeit if Rytsar ever came across him.

But what if… Rytsar thought to himself.

What if his father had the boy killed to eliminate evidence he was behind the kidnapping? If causing his son to commit suicide had been Vladimir's intent, he had come dangerously close to succeeding.

Tatianna had died by her own hands—her sweet soul broken after what she'd endured all those months—and Rytsar had seriously considered following her.

It was only his mother's suggestion that he leave for America that saved Rytsar's life back then. Leaving behind the memories and pain associated with Tatianna helped him refocus and start on a new path—a path that included his blood brother, Thane Davis.

Rytsar suddenly felt ice course through his veins as a new realization hit him.

Mamulya…

His mother had died only a few days after his return to Russia.

Rytsar was unable to stop the tears that welled in his eyes as he considered the terrible possibility.

"What is it?" Nikolay asked.

Rytsar shook his head. Surely his father could not be so cold-blooded as to kill his own wife, whom he was estranged from, but still loved fiercely.

"You should have let me kill him," Rytsar growled angrily.

"You already know why I could not."

Rytsar glared at Nikolay. "I am not grateful to be alive today. I owe you nothing but my rage at the injustice your interference has caused."

Raising an eyebrow, Nikolay replied, "I do not expect your gratitude."

"Then why am I here? What do you want from me?" Rytsar challenged.

"Your father is unworthy of the power your grandfather's inheritance will give him. I prefer it goes to the man it was meant for."

"Why would you care?"

"Like I said, your grandfather and I respected each other. My profound respect for him extends to you."

"Whether you like it or not, my father will die," Rytsar declared, his voice cold with rage.

Nikolay inclined his head. "As long as it's of natural causes, I have no issues."

Rytsar understood then that Nikolay was asking him to kill Vladimir quietly. "I will see to it that Vladimir Durov dies a slow, painful, and humiliating death—by natural causes, of course."

"Good."

Nikolay snapped his fingers and one of his men came into the room.

"Rytsar Durov must be leaving. See to it that he gets to his destination safely."

"Da, *Pakhan*."

Rytsar had to hold in his mounting rage as he was escorted out amid the hostile stares of the two Koslov brothers. Revenge was his only focus now. Instead of being driven to his home, Rytsar insisted that he be dropped off at Titov's apartment.

When Titov opened the door and saw who it was, he frowned. "I have nothing to say and seeing you only brings pain to me. Go away, Rytsar."

"I was wrong."

Titov was visibly taken aback by the bold statement and stared at him in silence.

"I was wrong to blame you for Tatianna."

"*Nyet,*" Titov replied, shaking his head. "My association with Yuri caused her death, and I will never forgive myself for it."

Rytsar could see the pain in Titov's eyes as he thought back on the tragic events leading up to his sister's death.

"Would you like to help me kill the man who *is* to blame?"

"What? Did you finally locate Yuri?"

"*Nyet.* I believe he is already dead."

"Who then?" Titov demanded.

"My father."

Titov took a step back, shocked by Rytsar's words. "What?"

"Not only is Tatianna dead because of my father, but now my mother is too."

"What is this? You're telling me that your mother is dead?" Titov asked, looking devastated.

"An assassin came last night as payment for my father's gambling debt. Does that sound familiar to you?"

Titov growled.

"*Da*," Rytsar replied, his voice choking up with emotion. "I have come to believe my father is responsible for both deaths."

"But why?" he demanded.

"Apparently, I am about to come into my grandfather inheritance, but my father lusts after it and can only receive it if I die."

"Why not simply kill you then?"

"Suicide is the only way it will revert to him, and there can be no hint I was murdered."

What Rytsar was telling him took time for Titov to process. He shook his head again, crying out, "But why my sister?"

Rytsar put his hand on Titov's shoulder. "We both know I considered following her after her death. It was a shrewd and heartless plan." Tears filled his eyes. "I now have lost the two most important women in my life because of him, and I demand revenge."

"Why are we standing on this doorstep talking? He

needs to die now!" Titov asserted.

Rytsar squeezed his shoulder, keeping him in place. "I tried to kill him last night, but was stopped by Nikolay."

"Why would the Koslovs care?" Titov snarled, fighting against Rytsar's firm grip.

"The brothers have granted my father their protection."

Titov froze, reality setting in. "But shouldn't you be dead then?"

"Nikolay spared my life because he agrees my father should die."

Knowing that they had the blessing of the Koslov *Pakhan*, Titov immediately asked, "What do you want me to do?"

Rytsar smiled—the kind of cruel smirk that mimicked his own father's. "I want you to get me some ricin."

"Poison? But I want to rip him apart limb by limb. Where is the satisfaction in that? I *need* him to feel my wrath," Titov growled.

Rytsar tightened his grip on his shoulder. "I understand, Titov. I promise that he will feel your wrath, but it must appear he died of natural causes. It is the only way Nikolay can condone his death without interfering."

Titov roared. "It's not good enough!"

Rytsar loosened his grip and gazed deep into Titov's eyes. "I promise you, it will be."

Letting out a ragged sigh, Titov said with resentment, "Fine, I trust you but I do not like it."

Rytsar let go of him, looking away as the scene of his

mother's violent death replayed in his mind, still too fresh to shut out.

He closed his eyes and let out an agonized groan.

Rytsar felt Titov's hand on him. "I'm so sorry to hear about the death of your mother. She was a kind woman and has been a comfort to our family through the years. I grieve with you."

Rytsar nodded, not willing to look at him as the tears fell.

"I hope someday, after justice has been dealt, I will finally be able to lead a normal life. Possibly we can even become friends again," Titov stated hopefully.

"It has been dark for far too long," Rytsar agreed, walking away from Titov without looking back.

Rytsar wanted revenge, yes, but without Tatianna and his sweet mother in his life, he didn't see the point of going on. His inheritance made little difference, death tasting far sweeter to him. The promise of money and power was a cold substitute for the ones he loved.

More than anything, he longed to be in their presence again…

Guardian Angel

Rytsar inadvertently let out a groan when the men dragged him off the plane.

"Is the coward finally awake?" the instigator asked expectantly.

Rytsar kept his eyes closed and didn't make another sound.

The leader quickly checked him over and announced, "He is still unconscious, but at least he survived the trip. We need to get him to the Koslov brothers before his health deteriorates any further, or it will be our heads on the line. Now be careful with him!" he ordered as Rytsar was lifted into the back of a van. "Secure him so that he doesn't roll about and injure himself further."

Rytsar barely endured the rutted dirt roads with the van's worn shock absorbers. His gut was racked with an excruciating pain on a level he'd never experienced.

This kind of pain did not bode well for him…

The only way he was able to keep silent was focusing all his energies on one thought—his need to hold the babe *moye solntse* in his arms. Even if he were truly dying, he would eke out every fucking breath until he held that little miracle.

The van stopped and the door slid open. Instead of being manhandled this time, he was treated with kid gloves as he was carried by several men. The cold Russian air was soon replaced with the warmth of a crackling fire as he was taken inside.

The leader spoke as they entered. "We have brought the merchandise."

"He's a fucking mess," Stas complained.

"It was not easy subduing him."

"The shit was a coward and insulted you," the instigator added.

"I do not care what he said," Stas replied coldly. "We charged you with delivering him and nothing more."

The leader quickly answered, "We had to muscle him down to subdue him, but he has been left untouched since."

Stas sounded unimpressed. "We cannot consider your mission a success unless he awakens." Rytsar felt the unwelcomed hands of Stas as he examined his body thoroughly, poking and prodding as he went about it. "Broken ribs, internal damage… You may have brought him here alive, but he is dying."

The overly confident voice of Gavriil filled the room. "Do not concern yourself, brother. Durov is too spineless to die."

"But how am I supposed to fuck with him if he doesn't regain consciousness?"

Gavriil laughed. "I'll show you how."

Rytsar heard the man walk out of the room and return a short time later. The buzzing electricity warned him what was coming before the cattle prod made contact with his stomach and the current shocked his damaged organs.

His eyes opened of their own accord as he began choking, blood bubbling up in his mouth.

"There you go," Gavriil said proudly to his brother. "Now you can have your fun."

Rytsar remained on the floor, choking on his own blood.

"Do something!" Stas demanded from the men who had brought him in.

A cloth was brought to Rytsar's mouth to wipe away the blood and then someone tried to force water down his throat. It only caused him to cough, aggravating the pain in his gut.

Rytsar stared straight ahead, imagining *moye solntse* as he commanded his body to relax. With great effort, he stopped coughing and lay there, his entire body streaming sweat as he involuntarily shivered.

"A pussy through and through," Stas gloated. "Look at the way he cowers before us."

Gavriil bent down and snapped Rytsar's head up. "The great Anton Durov, how does it feel to know you will be dying by our hands? My grandfather is no longer here to save your sorry *zhopa*."

Rytsar only glared at him, the pain rendering him speechless.

"I couldn't stand to hear my grandfather talk about you. You may have fooled him, but we know the truth. You couldn't even keep your woman and your own mother safe. You're destined to die a fatherless man, and your name will soon be forgotten."

Rytsar smiled.

"And now he grins like a fool," Stas said with a laugh.

"I think the big tough sadist is actually a masochist inside." Gavriil chuckled cruelly. Addressing Rytsar, he asked, "Anton, do you like it when I do this?"

A swift kick to his stomach had Rytsar coughing up blood again, but this time he could not stop it.

"Get him out of here," Stas demanded. "He is soiling the cashmere rug."

The men who had delivered him immediately picked him up and rushed him out of the room. They headed out the back and walked for several minutes until they came to a small cement building buried in the ground.

The iron door creaked as it was opened and he was dragged inside. Rytsar rolled into a ball to protect himself as the heavy door was closed and its lock slid into place.

"I highly recommend you don't die, Durov," the instigator called out to him, laughing as he walked away.

Rytsar closed his eyes as blood fell from his lips. He could feel his body closing down, preparing itself for the end. He couldn't stop the cold blackness as it began to envelop him.

However, he was not afraid. He longed to see Tatianna and his mother again—but he would die with regret.

Thinking of the promise he'd made to Brie, he whispered, "I am sorry, *radost moya…*"

His breaths came in ever shallower gasps, but he

fought for each and every one. Eventually, they came in further and further intervals until they finally stopped.

In the middle of the warm, inky abyss, he heard Brie scream out in anguish, her cry coming to him from a great distance.

"Rytsar!"

His eyes immediately popped open and he took in a ragged, painful breath.

The pain was excruciating, but he was grateful to be alive.

It was not his time—not yet.

Moving with immense effort, he positioned his body to better protect his torso from the unforgiving concrete.

He lay on the cement floor, unmoving in his buried concrete prison, unsure of the passage of time. His only source of reference was the small barred opening near the top of the ceiling. The window was too small for escape, but large enough to remind him that the days were continuing on without him.

Rytsar knew he was suffering from a severe fever and assumed it caused delirium, because he swore on several occasions someone had walked past the opening, but he was too weak to call out to them.

Days melded into one another as he lay there suffering in unspeakable agony. The Koslov brothers wanted him dead, but they also wanted it to be a lingering end. To ensure that happened, each day one of their henchmen came to force water down his throat.

Rytsar made sure to cry out in pain whenever he was touched. He needed everyone to believe he was on the verge of death even though he was slowly recovering. It was the only way he had any real chance of escape.

Encouraged by his recovery, Rytsar felt a surge of destiny when he noticed the shadow appear at the opening again. He called out, but his voice was too hoarse to be heard. Slowly drawing in his breath, he let out a low whistle instead.

He heard a whine and saw a black nose thrust its way between the bars.

Fuck! It was just a damn animal.

Rytsar groaned to himself in disgust.

The beast continued to sniff and whine, as if waiting for Rytsar to respond. He cursed the dog in Russian and told it to go away.

Instead of leaving, the animal began whining even louder. Rytsar tried to ignore the damn beast, but it refused to leave.

"Go home," Rytsar growled out painfully, needing it to obey him.

It seemed excited by Rytsar's attention and started turning in circles, its wagging tail hitting the bars as it circled itself.

"Fuck off," Rytsar barked, closing his eyes and rolling to face the wall. Maybe if he was quiet long enough the dog would take the hint and scram.

No such luck.

When the henchman entered the cell, Rytsar remained completely still.

He soon felt the kick of a boot in his lower back and momentarily saw stars from the pain it evoked.

"Roll over, you sack of shit," the man grumbled as he pulled roughly on Rytsar's shoulder, forcing him onto his back.

The dog began whining.

"Scat!" the man yelled up at the stray.

The whining grew louder as Rytsar's head was propped up and tepid water flowed into his mouth. His thirst demanded he gulp it, but Rytsar let some of the water dribble from his lips. This enraged his captor and he leaned his knee into Rytsar's side as he tilted the cup higher.

Water flowed from his chin and onto the floor. An unwanted waste, but necessary. As long as the Koslov brothers believed he was between life and death, he would have the freedom to observe and plan his flight.

But that damn dog would not shut up.

Rytsar saw the henchman take out his gun and point it at the beast. For reasons Rytsar could not fathom, he decided to intervene at the last second.

Flopping around violently, Rytsar pretended to choke on the water left in his mouth. His carefully orchestrated movements allowed him to kick the man in the knee, causing him to miss as the bullet ricocheted off the concrete, taking a chunk out instead.

"Fucking strays," the henchman snarled as he turned the gun on Rytsar's prostrate body. But without any authority to kill the prisoner, the man could only kick him in frustration.

"I hope you die soon," he hissed under his breath as

he walked out of the cell and locked the iron door.

Rytsar grabbed his side in agony after the lock slid into place. He was certain that his ribs had been rebroken with that final kick.

Sniffing sounds started from above as the dog returned, sticking its black nose through the bars. Thankfully, this time Rytsar was spared its constant whining. Maybe the dog understood its whining had put it in peril.

"You're going to get us both killed," Rytsar growled, rolling onto his uninjured side.

Fuck it, he was back where he'd started—struggling to suck in enough air with the shallow breaths he could manage.

Why he'd spared the mongrel he couldn't say, but it felt like a victory. He decided to name the nuisance *Glupyy*, the word for foolish.

"Scat, *Glupyy*…and don't come back."

Rytsar laid his cheek against the hard concrete and closed his eyes, ignoring the rumbles of an empty stomach as he kept tears of pain at bay.

The dog let out a low whine and then, to Rytsar's relief, it disappeared.

Rytsar let out a sigh, glad the beast had finally taken the hint. Maybe it would live to see another day.

The lack of food was causing him to drift in and out of consciousness. When he smelled the sea breeze and heard Brie's laughter, he smiled to himself, believing she was near.

"*Radost moya…*" he murmured huskily.

"Get up, you lazy aristocrat," Thane told him.

Rytsar opened his eyes and looked up at his old friend, who was holding a hand out to him.

"How long have I been sleeping?" Rytsar asked.

"Not long, but Brie's anxious to get started so I agreed it was time to wake your ass up."

Rytsar glanced over at Brie and smirked. "So you want me?"

She giggled in response. "I don't think that has ever been a question." Putting her hands on her hips, Brie said teasingly, "How long are you going to make me wait?"

He chuckled, taking Thane's hand and standing up.

Brushing off the sand from his body, Rytsar turned to face her. "Being a sadist, I think you know my answer."

Brie stuck out her bottom lip, giving him big doe eyes. "Please, Rytsar, do not make me wait any longer. Ever since you gifted this island to us, I have longed to scene with you here."

Hearing Brie speak of her desire for him naturally caused Rytsar's cock to stir. He let out a low growl. "I have waited far too long for this."

Thane clapped him on the shoulder. "As have we, old friend."

Rytsar looked back at Brie. Her playful smile melted his cold Russian heart and her body inspired his sadistic passions. "Undress for me," he commanded, longing to see her naked body again.

Brie nodded and, without hesitation, undid the strap of her white bikini top, letting it fall to the sand. She looked at Rytsar flirtatiously as she shimmied out of her bottoms and handed them to him.

He took a whiff of the alluring smell of her pussy lingering on the cloth and grunted. "I have missed your scent, *radost moya*."

"Miss me no more," she answered, opening her arms wide for a hug.

Rather than embrace her, Rytsar hiked her small frame over his shoulder and told Thane, "I aim to challenge this one today."

"Excellent," his comrade answered. "It's been a while since she's had a healthy challenge."

Brie cried out, "I'm not a masochist, I'm not a masochist!"

Rytsar chuckled with wicked amusement.

He knew she both loved and feared him—it was part of the reason he was so damn attracted to her. That combination would make today's play that much more stimulating, because he was serious about challenging her.

Rytsar walked her into the tiny home and set her on the ground. She struggled to keep her open submissive pose as he circled her, objectively noting the areas of her body he wanted to explore.

"Why are your eyes so big?" he teased, as he reached for his cat o 'nines.

She made a little squeak and looked to Thane.

He moved to her, lifting her chin with his finger and kissing her on the lips. "You have but to say your safeword at any point."

Brie gasped. "You want him to use his 'nines on me?"

"I desire to observe your session, as I was not present your first time. I am also curious to see how much you've grown, babygirl."

She glanced at Rytsar, now trembling as she smiled at him. "I *am* curious how much I can take since my first cat o 'nines."

His cock ached upon hearing those words. Now that he had both Thane and Brie's permission, he planned to put *radost moya* through her paces.

"*Moy droog*, bind her tight, spread-eagle. I don't want her able to wiggle out of my 'nines' caresses."

Rytsar stood back and watched with pleasure as his brother bound his trembling sub using rings screwed into the floor and suspended chain hanging from the ceiling. It gave him an unobstructed view to admire her form.

Brie's nipples were pert and erect, alerting him to her level of fear and anticipation. She also watched her Master intently as he tied her up. He was slow and meticulous, making sure the rope was taut and his ties secure so she was completely immobilized once he was finished.

Thane moved away from her, standing beside Rytsar. "I've never seen her this nervous before."

"It is intoxicating, isn't it?"

"I do enjoy bringing her to the edge of her endurance from time to time."

Brie kept her gaze straight ahead, trying to keep a brave face, but the shallowness of her breathing gave the truth away. It was endearing that she tried to hide it. But as always, Rytsar wanted his beautiful *radost moya* to experience both pleasure *and* pain.

The two of them began circling her, touching her in random places, leaving a kiss or a nibble as they teased her with their dual attention. Being unable to move, Brie was a slave to their seduction and fed on the sexual tension the two created.

She moaned in pleasure when Thane leaned in to kiss her while Rytsar pressed up against her back, the hardness of his cock resting between her butt cheeks.

Rytsar claimed the sensitive skin on the side of her throat as Thane kissed her deeply with his tongue. Their message clear—a spirited threesome would be her reward after the session.

Brie gasped as Rytsar bit down, wanting to mark her skin before he began to play.

When Thane pulled away, he followed suit, leaving Brie tied, fearful and helpless, before the two men.

"*Radost moya*, do you remember my three rules from the last time you and I played together at the cabin?" he asked her.

Brie nodded her head.

"Tell me," he commanded.

"First, I must be courageous. Second, I must be honest with you. And third, I need to trust you."

"*Da*. Do you still agree to these things?"

"Yes, Rytsar."

He smiled as he picked his 'nines back up and approached her.

Instantly, Brie tensed.

Rytsar glanced at his comrade and nodded in the direction of her tense back muscles. Thane raised an eyebrow, communicating his curiosity at how Rytsar would handle it.

He swung the wicked instrument in the air, letting Brie hear its dangerous promise as the knotted tails cut through the air, and was rewarded with her soft whimper.

Ah, such an alluring sound.

To begin the session, Rytsar chose to surprise Brie. He trailed his 'nines over her skin, starting with her arms and moving down her back. She shivered involuntarily, goosebumps rising on her skin. He grazed her shapely buttocks, slapping them ever so lightly with the knots, then he moved in front of her so that his 'nines could caress her beautiful breasts.

Brie shifted her gaze to him, knowing he preferred eye contact when they played together.

"Do you like my 'nines, *radost moya*?" he asked with a smirk.

"Right now, yes."

His chuckle was low and seductive, wanting her to appreciate his favorite instrument so she would invite the pain he longed to give her. He swiped one hand against her pussy and was pleased to find it wet.

"Your body is telling me it wants more. What does your mind tell you?"

She stared at his cat o 'nines for several moments

before lifting her head and looking into his eyes. "I am up for the challenge, Rytsar."

He leaned in and kissed her deeply, his cock straining against the material of his leather pants. "Let me guide you to *rai* then…"

When he stepped away, he could feel Brie's fear wash from her like waves of the sweetest ambrosia. She was courageous and she was willing despite her fear—this was her gift to him.

Taking his stance, Rytsar readied himself to deliver the first lash across her back. The seconds before that initial contact were a divine moment for him; a physical thrill as his body rushed with excitement.

He let his 'nines fly and closed his eyes in ecstasy when she let out that first sensual scream. His cock throbbed as he readied to deliver the next stroke. Brie was impressive this time around, taking his first round of four healthy strokes without calling her safeword.

While he paused for a moment to let her body prepare for the next set, Thane came to her, wrapping his hand around her throat and plundering her mouth. Tag-teaming her this way would help Brie to associate pleasure with the sting of the cat o 'nines. An association he hoped she would grow to crave given time.

"Ready for more?" he asked her, anxious to continue.

"*Da*, Rytsar," she said breathlessly when Thane released his hold on her.

Needing more from her, he gave her six strikes the second set, leaving red welts covering her back. Still she did not cry out her safeword, although the tears had started to flow.

"Impressive," he murmured seductively. Rytsar handed his 'nines to Thane to hold for a minute while he approached her, wanting to examine her red back.

So many love marks to count…

"Your endurance is inspiring, *radost moya*," he told her, pressing his hard cock against her body. "Do you feel how inspired I am?"

Brie looked up at him with tear-stained cheeks, attesting to her appreciation of his sadistic attentions. When she lifted her chin for a kiss, he grunted in satisfaction. It was a second level of submission—this acceptance of her desire and need to receive his pain.

Rytsar was not gentle as he claimed her mouth, wanting to ravage it with the same ferocity he wanted to ravage her entire body.

"The smell of you excites me," he confessed, noting a difference in her scent. It made him crazy for her, and he had to remind himself to hold back.

Brie was still a novice when it came to exploring the sensual world of pain with him. As much as he needed to feel her fear and hear her screams of delicious agony, he did not want her to become afraid of him.

"Are you ready for more?" he asked as he moved back into position.

Her whole body shook in an involuntary shiver, but she nodded her head yes.

Rytsar smiled at Thane. He understood this would be the last set, her body already so tense and resistant, she would struggle not to stop his 'nines' final caresses. But it was important to show her a hint of what she was missing, even if she was not quite able to appreciate it yet.

"Enjoy, *radost moya…*" he growled seductively as he let the knotted tails loose.

She threw her head back and let out a terrified scream as two more challenging consecutive lashes crisscrossed her back.

The two men descended on her at once, wanting to take her mind from the momentary feeling of terror the ferociousness of his 'nines had wrought.

With the pain came the pleasure…

They quickly unbound her, guiding her to the bed amid a volley of kisses and praises. She shifted her gaze between them both, unable to speak but responsive to every whisper, every kiss, every lick and nibble.

Rytsar and Thane worked together like a well-oiled machine as they brought her to her first orgasm after the session, forcing another scream from her.

"Do you think you could handle both of us at once as I minister to your back?" Rytsar asked lustfully, needing to feel his hard cock deep inside her and unable to wait.

"Yes," she begged.

While Thane grabbed her head to kiss her, Rytsar ran his hand over the smooth skin of her trembling stomach. But something was wrong.

He shook his head, trying to figure out what it was, feeling as if he was missing something.

Looking up at Brie, he cocked his head. "*Radost moya.*"

"Yes, Rytsar," she answered breathlessly, smiling

down at him.

Looking at her stomach again, he asked, "Where is the babe?"

Rytsar woke up to the chill of the cold night air. A shiver ran down his spine as he realized it had only been a dream. He groaned in pain as he moved to relieve the pressure on his side.

He heard whining above him.

The damn dog was back.

Unwilling to be tormented by its whining all night, he yelled, "Go!"

Rytsar saw movement in the dark as something fell from the opening. He heard it hit the cement a few feet in front of him.

The dog whined again.

The smell of meat met Rytsar's nostrils and his stomach growled in response, the hunger pains now impossible to ignore. He inched his way over until he could pick it up. It was a portion of cooked chicken, the smell of which drove him mad with hunger.

Brushing off the dirt and ignoring the fact it had been in the beast's mouth, Rytsar tore into the flesh and chewed with animal-like ferocity. It didn't take long for him to finish and he looked up at the outline of the dog's nose. "*Glupyy,* I need more." Rytsar could hear the dog's movement and had to assume it was wagging its tail vigorously.

"More," he called out again.

The dog disappeared, leaving Rytsar alone. He started nibbling on the thinner bones while he waited, ravenous for more.

It wasn't long before he felt the rush that protein caused as it flowed into his veins. He moaned in satisfaction, hope rising again from the power rush.

The stray returned a short time later with the back end of the bird. The dog nuzzled it through the bars until it fell into his cell. Rytsar grabbed the meat and began tearing at it, feeling as if he could never get enough. After he finished the last of it, he looked up again and crooned to the animal. "You have done well, *Glupyy*."

The dog whined softly in response.

Wanting the beast to know he was truly pleased, Rytsar said, "Good dog."

The sound of vigorous movement above let him know the dog was wagging its tail excessively. Rytsar smirked to himself. At least the beast was easy to please.

From that point on, *Glupyy* came to him only at night delivering scraps—the dog appeared to be the master of thieves. On the rare nights it couldn't find anything, the dog provided Rytsar with companionship. The animal gave him comfort by just being there with him, especially during those times when the pain became too great and the night too dark.

Rytsar was certain that Thane was doing everything possible to release him from this hell, but he prayed his comrade would fail. Anyone making the mistake of a rescue attempt would die a similarly torturous death. The

Koslov brothers would not suffer interference, and Rytsar could not stomach any more deaths on his account.

Titov understood the danger and, although he had been willing to stand beside Rytsar and die with him, he respected Rytsar's wish that he carry on and make sure Thane, Brie, and the babe were kept safe in the years ahead.

Titov understood that promise meant far more to Rytsar than sacrificing himself in solidarity.

Rytsar chuckled to himself thinking about Titov. There was no doubt in his mind that his longtime companion had a bottle of vodka and shot glass waiting for him even now. It would remain where it was up until the day Rytsar arrived to drink with him or Titov drew his last breath. He was not a man to break a promise.

Tatianna would have been proud of her older brother.

Rytsar wiped away an obnoxious tear.

Despite the tragedies he'd suffered, he had been blessed to know exceptional people. People worth fighting and dying for.

"*Glupyy,* how do you find yourself in such a sad predicament—nursing an ungrateful Russian? I'm curious if you were the pet of a soldier who has died or were you always a stray fighting for survival."

The dog made a happy little woof and turned in circles.

Mamulya

The sweet lullaby his mother used to sing to him as a little boy lingered in Rytsar's mind as he tried to fall asleep. It gave him comfort—that haunting melody sung in his mother's beautiful voice:

Darkness is falling,
The moon will be rising
The stars will be shining
The sun's gone to sleep
Close your eyes
And I'll rock you gently
And wish you sweet dreams
While you sleep
Good night,
Good night
Now it is time to sleep

Tears came to his eyes, the memories of his youth flooding back, the period before the whipping pole and his introduction to pain and the cruelty of his father at the tender age of five.

As a young boy, he'd loved to sit in the kitchen and watch his mother cook. Although she could have had the staff do it, she'd insisted she be the one to feed her family.

She smiled down at her son as she divided the large dough into small balls to make her delicious Russian *pirozhkis.* "Anton, what do you want to be when you grow up?"

"An astronaut!" he answered with confidence.

"Ah, a brave man who explores the heavens."

Rytsar sat up straighter and puffed out his chest proudly.

He watched as she pinched off two small pieces of the dough and handed him one. "I have always loved the sweet taste of yeast in raw dough," she confessed.

He grinned, grabbing it from her with his small hand and popping it into his mouth. He agreed with her, it was a special treat whenever she made bread and was part of the reason he enjoyed sitting in the kitchen when she cooked.

As they chewed the dough, Rytsar was struck with a thought. "*Mamulya,* what did you want to be when you were little like me?"

"I've always wanted to be a teacher," she said, her smile widening.

His eyes grew big. "A teacher?"

"*Da.*"

"Are you sad?"

"Why?" she asked, tilting her head charmingly, her

delicate eyebrows raised in interest.

"You are not in a classroom."

His mother laughed softly as she began rolling out the small balls of dough. "I may not be in a traditional classroom, but I have you five boys to teach every day."

Rytsar grinned at her, happy she was content to simply be their mother.

"When you fly up in the rocket, I will be with you in spirit," she told him, rubbing the top of his head. "I've always wanted to see our blue planet from space."

"Me too!" he piped up, watching her carefully spoon the seasoned meat, onion, and egg mixture onto each circle of dough before she folded them over and crimped the edges. He skootched his chair closer to the stove so he could watch her fry them.

"Keep a safe distance," she reminded him gently.

"Yes, *Mamulya*," he answered, his mouth already watering as she placed the first one into the hot oil. The smell of frying bread filled the kitchen as she set each one into the large pot and turned them, making sure they were golden brown on both sides.

She placed the cooked *pirozhkis* in a basket to drain. Rytsar was sorely tempted to grab one, but had learned from experience that to do so was folly. He would only end up burning his tongue and not be able to taste his mother's delicious meat pies.

When enough time had passed for them to cool down, she handed him one. "I want you to grow into a strong man like your father and grandfather."

He chomped down on the crunchy bread and moaned in pleasure as he chewed the savory bite.

Speaking with his mouth still full, he answered, "I will be stronger, *Mamulya*."

His father walked into the kitchen just in time to hear the last of their conversation. "Stronger than your father? Hah!" he replied, taking a *pirozhki*. He looked accusingly at his wife. "How can he become a strong man when you baby him like a girl?"

"I am not a girl!" Rytsar protested.

"Well, you may not be wearing an apron like your mother, but boys don't play in the kitchen."

Rytsar was offended and frowned at his father. "I love *Mamulya*."

His father ripped a bite out of the meat pie and ate it, staring at him. After he swallowed, he said, "Growing into a mama's boy, are you?"

"I'm not a mama's boy."

"Vladimir," his mother said, wiping her hands on her apron before placing them on his chest, and looking up at him. "All of your sons are strong men, just like their father."

He gave Rytsar a sideways glance. "I don't like seeing him in the kitchen."

She smiled sweetly. "What harm does it do? We talk about important things while I cook. The time is not wasted."

"Still, the kitchen is not a place for a son of mine."

Rytsar's mother handed him another *pirozhki*, saying in a sweet voice, "Did you never spend time in the kitchen, getting treats from your mother while she cooked? I believe those extra morsels are how you grew up to be so big, strong, and handsome."

He smiled down at his wife lustfully, taking a large bite of her pie. "I want you in the basement right now, woman."

Mamulya bowed her head, taking off her apron, folding it neatly before laying it on the counter. She winked at Rytsar as she walked out of the kitchen, telling him, "Only one more, my little astronaut. I don't want you to spoil your dinner."

Rytsar could not stop the tears as he thought back on that sweet moment that was countered by the surprised look on her face as her life blood spilled onto the floor when she took her last breath.

She'd deserved so much more from life. Why fate had been so brutal to such a kind soul was a complete mystery to him.

Rytsar thought back on the day after her death. He'd spoken to Titov about revenge, and then headed directly to his brothers. Although they had gone their separate ways after reaching adulthood, they were still his family and needed to know the truth about their mother's death.

"I don't believe it," Vlad, his oldest brother, stated.

Pavel, the youngest, whose eyes were red from crying spoke up, insisting, "Father would never hurt Mama."

"What possible reason would he do such a thing?" Andrev asked, sneering at Rytsar. "This was clearly a hit by the Koslovs."

Even Timur, the most reasonable of his brothers, did not believe him.

"Money," Rytsar snarled angrily. "She died because our father is a greedy bastard."

"That makes no sense. Our father is a rich man," Vlad told him, defending the wretch.

"There are rumors floating around that Father is amassing a huge debt because of his gambling addiction," Timur offered, looking at Rytsar.

"I confronted the Koslovs last night, Timur," he answered. "I planned to kill Father with my own hands—"

"It is a cold day in hell when a son attacks his own flesh and blood," Andrev interrupted, shaking his head in disgust.

Rytsar told them, "Grandfather passed our father over when he allotted the Durov inheritance. He killed her wanting to get it back."

"What? Do the Koslovs have it now?" Pavel asked in concern.

"No, you *doorak,*" Vlad hissed, glaring at Rytsar. "Grandfather always had a favorite." He looked down at the ring on Rytsar's finger. "But why didn't Father just kill you if he wanted it so badly? He loves our mother."

"What? Are you saying Anton has all the money?" Andrev cried in anger.

"I don't have it yet," Rytsar told Andrev, before addressing Vlad. "He cannot get it by killing me."

Pavel shook his head. "None of this is making sense." Tears welled up in his eyes. "Mama is dead…why are we fighting?"

"Because our father was the one who killed her," Rytsar growled. "Why don't any of you care? He needs to die."

Andrev looked at him suspiciously. "What if this is some crazy scheme of yours to steal his inheritance?"

"Why would I do that?" Rytsar demanded.

"Because you hate Father, you always have," Andrev declared.

"Do I hate the man who had me beaten as a boy? Of course I fucking do, but I would never want him dead unless he hurt someone close to me—to all of us."

"Your accusations are unfounded," Vlad claimed.

"Nikolay all but confirmed them while I was there. It's the only reason I'm still alive."

Timur looked at Rytsar thoughtfully but said nothing.

"I refuse to believe Father did this," Pavel snarled.

Andrev scowled at Rytsar, then spat. "Everyone always favored you. Mama, Grandfather…even Father, and now you want to kill him."

"Are you insane, Andrev? I would have traded places with you in a second rather than being forced to suffer Father's sadistic brand of 'affection'."

"In the end, our mother is gone. Nothing we do will bring her back," Timur stated.

Rytsar shook his head in disbelief. "What is wrong with you? You all want to let Father live after what he did to our sweet mother?"

"As I said," Vlad replied in a cold voice, "what you are proposing is pure speculation. How unjust would it be if we killed our father and you were wrong?" He lifted his chin, giving Rytsar a superior look. "I think you have held on to your resentment for so long that you are blinded by it."

"I am not seeking revenge for myself. This is for *Mamulya.* Do none of you care?" Rytsar cried, horrified by the passivity of his brothers.

Pavel sniffled, wiping away his tears. "Of course we care, and we want to honor Mother as she would have wanted. We all need to grieve her loss as a family. Don't ruin this for us."

"Would you seriously stand beside Father knowing he was the reason she died such a violent death?"

"In this case, it's your word against his. I personally would believe Father over you," Vlad answered.

Timur looked sadly at Rytsar. "Brother, we must unite as a family. I don't want to hear any more discussion about Father murdering Mama. It is cruel and untrue."

"Timur," Rytsar exclaimed, "don't turn a blind eye to the truth. It's not fair to *Mamulya*."

"There will be a service for Mama tomorrow. You are not invited to join us," Andrev announced.

His brothers all nodded.

Rytsar backed away from them, horrified by the turn of events. They were all sniveling cowards, just like Vladimir. It seemed he was the only one with a backbone and a sense of justice.

"I would never stand with you in mourning. You are all dead to me."

That was the last Rytsar saw of his brothers, other than that one time he went out of his way to help Andrev and was stabbed in the back—a bitter betrayal he could never forget or forgive.

It turned out his brothers were as spineless as Vladimir, the only real difference being that they had not inherited his sadism as well. No, it had been passed down to Rytsar, and he had no trouble dealing out the kind of justice his father deserved.

He'd never admitted to another person, not even to Thane, the hideous truth about his father or the true manner in which Vladimir finally met his maker.

Rytsar's thoughts were interrupted by the unexpected visit of Stas. The door swung open and he breezed into the room, smiling. "What do we have here? Wait. Are those tears I see?"

Turning his head away, Rytsar grunted in pain to cover up the fact they were tears of emotion.

"I kept getting reports you are on the verge of dying, so I had to come see for myself." He gave a prodding kick to Rytsar's back. "Turn and face me."

Rytsar did as he was told with exaggerated movements amid groans of pain.

"You really are a mess." Stas laughed unkindly. "Look at that face, still swollen and lumpy. And that stomach…I don't think the dark purple hue bodes well for you."

Rytsar said nothing as he grimaced in mock pain, his eyes downcast.

"You are nothing like I remember. The great Anton Durov, defender of the weak, because frankly, you look quite weak yourself—just like your father."

"Leave…my father out of this," Rytsar grunted.

Stas laughed. "What a worthless piece of shit he was too. Couldn't even make things work to get his inheritance back." He muttered to himself, "It's not like we didn't try to help his cause…"

Rytsar glanced up at him, trying not to show the rage

now building in his heart for Stas. So the truth was finally out. The brothers had personally sent the assassin to kill his mother at the request of his father. Just one more reason the Koslov brothers needed to die.

"Hungry…" Rytsar whimpered, wanting to appear as weak and pathetic as Stas assumed.

Stas dug in his pocket and threw him a piece of *vzletnaya*, a hard lemon candy. "Try that," he encouraged. "It should help."

Rytsar didn't trust the man, and felt something odd was up with Stas. When he didn't move to pick up the candy, Stas suddenly became irate. "I give you what you ask for and you don't even have the decency to take it?" He scooped the candy off the floor and unwrapped it, bending down to force it into Rytsar's mouth, then clamped his jaw shut. With a glint in his eye, Stas watched Rytsar struggle as he choked on the lemon candy, the citrus flavor further drying out his already parched mouth.

"There, that's better," Stas stated in a pleased voice once Rytsar forced the candy down. "I wouldn't want you to have bad breath when I do this." Before Rytsar knew what was happening, he felt Stas's firm lips on his.

Rather than reacting with a swift kick to the groin, Rytsar stayed still, allowing the unwanted contact. He had to maintain his ruse until the timing was right.

"Come on, you bad boy, kiss me…" Stas said, pressing his tongue against Rytsar's closed lips.

"Oh hell."

Stas stiffened upon hearing his brother's voice, as Gavriil walked into the cement enclosure.

Breaking away, Stas laughed callously as he stood up. "I wanted to check his breath to make sure he's still alive."

Gavriil did not seemed fooled by what he'd just witnessed. "When you said you wanted to fuck with Durov, I never thought you actually meant you wanted to *fuck* him."

"Don't be an ass. I was just checking him out," Stas said defensively.

"I could *see* that."

Stas sucker-punched Gavriil in the face, causing the older brother to fall to the cement floor. Rytsar was about to make his move against the two when three other men entered the cell, alerted by the commotion.

Gavriil jumped to his feet and wiped the blood from his nose, roaring, "If you ever touch me again, I'll fucking kill you!"

"Did the prisoner do this?" Ivan, Rytsar's 'caretaker' blurted, ready and anxious to end Rytsar.

"*Nyet*," Gavriil growled, kicking at Rytsar's still body. "We wasted our time bringing Durov here. He's useless as a dead man. Go get the men who delivered him to us. Tell them I am not happy."

Rytsar silently laughed. The Koslov brothers were making his job easier by eliminating those men. It meant less work for him. Now he could concentrate on the brothers themselves. The men who had a direct hand in his mother's death.

Freedom

Rytsar laughed out loud when he saw that black nose. It had become their nightly ritual now—two outcasts commiserating together in the dark. He picked up the sausage link the dog had pushed through the opening, chomping on it gratefully. Meat was a powerful weapon for the body when healing.

Rytsar knew he'd lost considerable weight, but because of the dog's diligence, he had maintained muscle.

"It won't be long now," Rytsar told the dog. "Do not be upset when you come here one night and I am gone. It will be a good thing, and it means you won't have to scavenge for me."

Glupyy danced in a circle, wagging its tail.

Rytsar thought of *moye solntse* and smiled to himself. He'd been thinking of her more and more as his health slowly improved.

"When I leave here, I will be going to America. Do you know why?" he asked the animal.

Glupyy responded by sticking its nose through the bars and sniffing.

"There's a babe I am destined to meet. I believe it's the reason you came to me. You are part of a greater plan, little pup."

The dog let out a gentle woof, which was unusual for the animal. Rytsar took it as a sign that *Glupyy* agreed with him.

But suddenly, the dog disappeared.

A moment later, Rytsar heard footsteps in the gravel path leading up to his cell. He tensed, unsure if his rescue was at hand—or his death.

The lock clanked as it was slid back and the iron door creaked loudly as it opened. Rytsar watched as a hand holding a pistol appeared first while the person slowly entered the room alone.

"Durov, we have unfinished business," Stas said, inching toward him.

Rytsar kept still on the floor.

"I know you're awake. I heard you talking. Do you normally talk to yourself?"

Rytsar paused before speaking, making it sound as if he were laboring for his breath. "It keeps me…sane," he finally croaked.

Stas towered above him, looking down, a black silhouette of a man except for the barrel of the gun pointed at Rytsar's head. "You know what I want from you."

Rytsar looked up, feeling that odd vibe again, his hackles now up. "*Nyet.*"

"I want you to kiss me, and let me touch you."

Bile rose in Rytsar's mouth.

Stas slowly lowered himself to kneel beside Rytsar.

Images of what had happened to him in college suddenly sprang in Rytsar's mind. That night Samantha had taken his drunk ass upstairs to his dorm room, only to tie him up and spend the rest of the evening abusing him with his own instruments in an ungodly and intoxicated power play to dominate him.

The maggot before him now was going to die. No one would *ever* violate his body again.

As if Stas could read his thoughts, Rytsar felt the end of the barrel pressed against his groin. "This time I want you to kiss me like you mean it. Anything less, and I will be forced to shoot your manhood off. Now wouldn't that be a shame?"

Rytsar watched as Stas lowered his mouth within a few centimeters of his.

"Open," Stas commanded.

Opening his lips invitingly, Rytsar immediately bit down hard when Stas's tongue entered his mouth. The man screamed in pain as he tried to pull away. Rytsar fought for the gun but in the struggle, the weapon slipped from his hand and skidded across the floor.

Stas covered his mouth, blood dripping from it, screeching in rage. Rytsar eyed the door but knew he would have to take care of Stas first before he escaped. Standing up, he faced the younger Koslov brother with an evil smile, the berserker in him ready to rumble.

Light flooded the cell as men marched in, guns drawn.

"That is enough!" Gavriil barked. He looked at his brother in disgust before addressing Rytsar. "We are done here. *You're* done."

In that moment, Rytsar realized everything he'd been

fighting for was about to be lost. He stared at the numerous guns pointed at his heart and a feeling of defeat washed over him.

"*Nyet*," Gavriil said, seeming slightly amused. "A firing squad is too good for you. There's a storm coming. The temperatures are going to drop below freezing and you will die by the hands of mother Russia herself—in a cold and deadly embrace."

He turned back to his brother. "As for you, I hope you've finally learned your lesson."

His brother mumbled his words, difficult to understand. "He most bi my ong off…"

"Yes, he did, *doorak*. You don't play with mongrels or you might get bit." Gavriil laughed unsympathetically.

The men lowered their guns one by one as they exited the room, then the iron door was closed and locked for a final time.

I'm going to die here.

The cold reality of that statement had Rytsar sinking to his knees. All his suffering had been for nothing. He looked up toward the heavens in disbelief, a lone tear running down his cheek.

Just as Gavriil had promised, just before first light the bitter cold arrived. Rytsar sat in the corner of the cell shivering. Because the building was underground, the cement beneath him still retained some of the heat of the earth, but it was slowly becoming as cold as the air around him.

He heard the pup's cry and looked up. "I'm done for. Go save yourself."

The dog paced back and forth for several minutes as

if deciding what to do before it laid its body lengthwise against the bars. Rytsar wasn't sure what it was doing, but got the feeling it did not want him to die alone.

He was deeply moved by that and stood up, reaching up to touch the scroungy mutt for the very first and last time.

Rytsar felt a deep connection the moment his touched the animal. In response, the dog began licking him excitedly with its warm tongue as if it felt it too. Rytsar petted its fur for several minutes, studying it, overwhelmed by the sense of love the animal had for him.

The dog was an average-size mutt covered mostly in light brown scruffy hair, with a smoky gray muzzle and ears, as well as small patches above each eye giving the illusion of eyebrows. The unique coloring made the animal's face more expressive when it stared at him with those soulful eyes.

Eventually, he ordered *Glupyy* to leave, although the animal ignored his command.

Rytsar settled back down on the floor, curling up in a ball to conserve heat. If he must die, there were worse ways to go.

With the passage of time the painful shivering finally stopped as the numbness of hypothermia set in. He looked down at his hands, grateful they'd finally stopped aching even though he knew what it meant.

Hands…he thought dully.

The word made him think of Tatianna's delicate hands. He grunted in sadness.

Rytsar had blocked the memory, but it came back to

him full force without his permission, his mind too numb to stop it.

After five months of tracking her, Titov and Rytsar finally found Tatianna in a dilapidated building in the Ukraine with over twenty other young girls being housed for prostitution.

They found her huddled in a corner, her clothes threadbare and worn, barely covering the skeleton she'd become. He didn't realize she was drugged until Titov approached her.

At first, Tatianna flinched when he drew close, but then she looked up at him, her eyes glazed and her speech slurred. "Please…be gentle, mister." She lifted the hem of her shirt, exposing her naked body underneath the dress to him.

"*Nyet*, Tatianna," Titov cried out, pulling her dress back down and trying to embrace her.

She backed away, looking terrified of him.

"Tatianna, it's me," Rytsar called out, his voice warm and calming despite the fact his heart was breaking. She was a tragic vision with needle marks up her arm and bruises covering her small body. "It's okay, I am here now," he assured her.

Slowly the light of recognition began to shine in her eyes. She looked to Rytsar and then her brother. Instead of relief, she looked even more tormented. "Don't look at me," she cried, huddling in the corner and crouching down, trying to hide from them as she covered her face in her hands.

Rytsar looked at Titov, their expressions mirroring each other—one of defeat knowing they hadn't been able to save her from this hell.

As Rytsar approached, he noticed the fingers on her left hand had been broken. He shook his head, anger welling up inside him. However, he kept a calm exterior because he knew right now she needed tenderness not rage.

"We've come to take you home," Titov told her.

She spread her fingers wide enough to look up at him. "Home?" she repeated, her voice wavering with emotion.

"Yes, my little sparrow."

Her bottom lip trembled as she gazed into Rytsar's eyes.

"Anton…"

She reached out to him, her arms shaking as tears filled her eyes.

"I'm here, Tatianna. No one will hurt you again." Rytsar lifted her up and wrapped his arms around her tiny skeletal form. She was so fragile…

Tatianna shook her head as she pressed herself against him, unable to speak.

Titov stood back from them, his countenance one of relief and devastation.

Rytsar tried not to squeeze her too hard, but he longed to keep her forever in his protective embrace. They stayed together holding each other, bonded in silence, until he looked down at her mangled hand.

"Why did they do this?" he growled in anger.

She looked up at him with those crystal blue eyes, defiance burning in them. "They tried to take your ring from me."

Tatianna held up her damaged hand, several fingers misshapen from being broken and healing at odd angles. His ring hung loosely on her thumb now, her fingers too thin for it.

"I couldn't let them have it," she told him fervently. "This ring was my only connection to you—my only hope."

Rytsar crushed her to him, unable to breathe.

If only it had been enough…

He opened his eyes, finding himself back in the cell with frozen tears on his face. Oh God, how it hurt knowing she had ended her life, too broken by what had happened to her.

Rytsar's only solace was that she had died in her own home, surrounded by people who loved her, even though it hadn't been enough to save her.

Now he could rejoin Tatianna, and kiss away that pain for an eternity.

The dog let out a soft woof before disappearing, alerting him that someone was coming. Rytsar slowly turned his head toward the door and waited.

The lock slid back and two of Koslov's men walked inside.

"What, have you decided to put me out of my misery?" Rytsar asked jokingly.

"Shut up," Ivan barked, grabbing his right arm while the other man grabbed his left. They dragged him out of the cell—his private hell for an unknown number of weeks.

Whether he lived or died, at least he was free.

Rytsar was dragged through the freshly fallen snow just as the sun peeked over the horizon. A new day had dawned and he was still a part of it.

He was taken back into the house and, to his relief, deposited next to a roaring fire in the fireplace.

Even though the pain was unbearable as his limbs slowly began to thaw from the numbing cold, he knew it meant life. He could endure anything as long as he was given the chance to fulfill his promise to *radost moya* and the babe.

The Koslov brothers came into the room hours later, neither of them looking happy. Stas stared at him in fear, an ice pack wedged in his mouth to keep down the swelling of his tongue.

Rytsar liked that look on him.

Gavriil said nothing, his seething anger palpable.

It was a mystery to Rytsar why he was here now, when it was obvious neither brother wanted this.

Oh hell…

Had Thane orchestrated a ransom? If so, what had he sacrificed to spare Rytsar's life?

Rytsar closed his eyes, now more concerned than ever. Whoever came to deliver the ransom was in peril. The brothers were obviously upset, even though they had agreed to the exchange.

Just one wrong word or look, and the notoriously irrational Koslov brothers could fly off the handle, killing everyone.

Rytsar heard a commotion deep inside the building and the cry of a woman. He tensed, listening to the scuffle as it continued. Although he was certain it wasn't Brie, the woman's scream heralded the arrival of his "rescue" party.

How he hoped they all made it out alive.

Before negotiations began, Rytsar was pulled unceremoniously onto a chair and ordered not to move as they tied his wrists to the arms of it.

Now all he could rely on was his ability to talk them through the situation, hoping it would be enough. But Gavriil did not trust Rytsar, and took that away from him as one of the men gagged him with a strip of cloth.

Stas handed the bloody ice pack to one of the men and told him to get rid of it as he faced the door, hands behind his back and a look of hatred on his face.

Rytsar stared at the door, his heart pounding as the footsteps of several people drew nearer. Who would come through that door?

Rytsar watched as three people he knew were pushed into the room and thrown to the floor.

He was shaken to his very core when he looked into the bloody faces of Captain, Wallace, and the last person he ever expected to see—Samantha.

Rytsar glared at them heatedly, livid they had ignored his warnings and risked their lives to save him.

Now their blood would be on his hands as well.

Gavriil said tauntingly, "Do they seem familiar to you, worm?"

Rytsar grunted angrily in answer, turning his head from them in disgust.

Stas chuckled but kept his mouth shut to hide his injury.

"American fools," Gavriil stated. "They have risked their lives for you. I wonder why they would do that." He turned to face Rytsar, smirking. "Hmm?"

Gavriil placed his heavy boot on Samantha's back and leaned down, placing the barrel of his gun against her temple. "What would you do if I shot her right now?" He then laughed, stating, "Nothing. Because there is nothing *you* can do, is there?"

Stas looked down at Samantha and cleared his throat to get Gavriil's attention. When he had it, he glanced at Samantha again wearing an unreadable expression it seemed only Gavriil understood.

Gavriil slowly removed his foot. "Wait. Is this the infamous Mistress Clark? The woman who humiliated Durov in every possible way known to man? Stas is quite the admirer of yours." He chuckled as he held out his hand to her. "My sincerest apologies, Mistress."

Samantha took his hand, the red mark on her cheek highlighting the way she had been treated. But she stood up with grace and power, an aura of confidence. "I am one and the same," she answered coolly.

Gavriil turned to Rytsar. "These heathens might not be here for your rescue after all. How curious…"

He turned back to Samantha and demanded, "Why have you come?"

"We are here to retrieve Durov," she replied with smooth conviction.

"For what purpose?"

"Does that matter? We have what you asked for."

"We did not offer any exchange to you," he huffed, lifting his gun and pointing it at her head.

Samantha remained unruffled as she explained, "My colleagues and I are here on behalf of Vlad Durov. The man you made the offer to. He will be extremely unhappy when he finds out the manner in which we have been treated."

"I don't believe you," Gavriil scoffed. "Vlad would *never* align himself with a woman."

All the men in the room chuckled in agreement.

"As he already informed you, Vlad is unwilling to dirty his hands with this mess but I, on the other hand, have no such qualms. Rest assured, I *am* here on his behalf and I can prove it to you." She nodded toward the door. "Except one of your men stole the timepiece I was instructed to hand to you."

Gavriil seemed appeased by her answer and nodded to Stas who left the room to retrieve it.

While they waited, Gavriil looked the Domme over appreciatively. "You are quite a looker, Mistress Clark. While I'm no bitch like Durov, I wouldn't mind showing you a taste of Russian hospitality." He moved in close and growled lustfully. "Let me show you what a real man does with American pussy."

Samantha raised her eyebrow, looking at him with disdain. "Mr. Koslov, I would break every bone in your body if you dared to try." She glanced down at Captain and Wallace dismissively and smiled. "Just ask my men."

"Ah…" Gavriil said in admiration. "So these are *your* men, not the other way around."

"Of course not. I bow to no man."

He moved in a little closer and said in a seductive tone, "I bet I could make you bow."

Stas walked in holding the item in his hand, but Gavriil ignored him.

Strolling over to Rytsar, he grinned down at him. "Tell me, worm. How does it feel to have no one on your side? We know what your father wanted to do to you. He recounted it many times to us in great detail. I assume his oldest son, who carries that same hatred for you, must have similar plans." Gavriil's eyes shone with excitement. "You kept that inheritance to yourself, being the selfish prick that you are. Brothers shouldn't act like that." He looked over at Stas and smiled. "I guess the time has come to pay for your mistakes at the hand of your eldest brother who was named after your father. It seems fitting, really."

He looked over at Stas. "Don't you agree, brother?"

Stas stared at Rytsar with a smug expression and then nodded to his brother, a slight grin on his lips. Rytsar had to admit that Stas was acting every bit the arrogant bastard he was, despite his recent injury.

Rytsar glared back at him, making a silent vow that Stas would die with a surprised look on his face—just as *Mamulya* had.

Gavriil laughed. "I remember your brother Vlad told me you were a real momma's boy as a child. Always crying and pulling on your mother's skirt, demanding her attention."

Rytsar rolled his eyes.

Gavriil did not care for that cavalier attitude, and leaned down, asking loudly as he glanced at Samantha,

"Tell me. How did it feel to take a dildo in the ass for this woman, while she crushed your balls in her hand?"

Rytsar looked up at him, now deciding how Gavriil would die.

"That's what I imagine happened," Gavriil said, chuckling. Looking to Samantha, he asked, "Am I right?"

She gave him a wicked smirk, saying haughtily, "Something like that."

Gavriil's laughter filled the room as he grinned at his brother.

As much as Rytsar hated Samantha, he admired the way she was playing the two brothers. She had them eating out of her hand, and they were completely oblivious to it.

"Let's finish this up, shall we?" Samantha said in a bored voice. "I may even overlook the grievous way you've treated me and my boys if you make this quick."

Samantha looked down at Captain and Wallace and ordered, "Stand up."

The Koslovs did not stop them as both men got to their feet, giving Rytsar a full view of the bloody marks they wore after being beaten by Koslovs' men.

It made Rytsar's blood boil, but instead of showing the brothers his anger, Rytsar narrowed his eyes, looking at Wallace and Captain with distrust as he tried to analyze how to take them down. It was essential he keep up the pretense of being enemies if they had any hope of getting out alive.

He refused to have the blood of these three on his hands.

"Vlad agreed to the payment?"

Samantha looked at him scornfully. "Would we be here if he hadn't?"

Gavriil told Stas, "Check the account to verify the transfer has been made."

Stas was forced to leave the room, the location of their compound so remote that communications were rudimentary and archaic. It was part of the appeal of this inhospitable area, making it the perfect spot for people to disappear without a trace.

Rytsar remained extremely concerned for their safety, fearful Stas would not let them go. Nothing was guaranteed until they were safely away from this place.

While they waited, Gavriil tried to flirt with Samantha, which she thwarted. His unsuccessful attempts seemed to turn him on even more. By the time Stas returned, Gavriil was sporting a noticeable hard-on.

Stas walked into the room and nodded to Gavriil.

"That is wonderful news, brother," Gavriil said with a smile. He looked at Samantha lustfully and offered, "Would you like me to kill my men who hurt you? I don't want there to be any hard feelings between us."

She glanced down at his bulging crotch, her face stoic as she answered, "Don't bother. There's nothing hard between us."

He smirked, obviously enjoying her insult, eager for more.

But Rytsar could tell Stas was not as equally mesmerized by Samantha as his brother, because he kept staring at Rytsar with a possessive look in his eye.

That look caused the hairs to rise on the back of Rytsar's neck.

The Sacrifice

"The deal is done then," Gavriil announced, sticking out his hand to shake Samantha's, but instead of shaking it, he grasped her hand, turned it and brought it to his lips.

Samantha jerked her hand away, telling Captain and Wallace, "Untie Durov. No need to be gentle with the merchandise."

Just as Captain began untying his bonds, Stas waved Gavriil over and whispered in his ear.

A chill went down Rytsar's spine.

"Wait," Gavriil suddenly stated. "Stas has brought up an excellent point. It is not right that Durov leave here without a sacrifice."

"What do you mean?" Samantha demanded, narrowing her eyes in suspicion.

"He killed a member of our family. There must be restitution."

"Isn't that what the ransom is for?" she insisted.

"No, an attack on the Koslovs as grievous as this requires a physical restitution be made. Something we can give to the family."

"Meaning?" Samantha asked, her voice cold as ice.

"An eye for an eye."

Samantha frowned menacingly, stating, "No, that was not part of the ransom."

"And yet, he will not leave until we have a sacrifice and we will not accept it from the worm himself." He smiled warmly at Captain and Wallace. "Which means it must come from one of you."

Rytsar snarled, struggling violently in his bonds, hoping to draw attention back to himself. He understood why they were demanding it from another. The Koslovs knew his history as a child. It would be far harder to watch someone else pay for his actions than to have it done to himself—he had been the whipping boy after all.

But he was ignored by Stas as he produced a large knife and moved toward the two men.

Rytsar's muffled howls filled the room when Stas approached Captain. He stopped and gave the man a closed-mouth grin as he tapped the leather patch covering Captain's left eye with the knife. He then slowly moved the blade, setting the tip against the edge of his right eyeball.

Captain did not flinch, looking Stas in the eye.

"I'll do it."

Stas smiled, turning to face Wallace. He moved over to the boy and stared deep into both his blue eyes as if deciding which one he would take.

Samantha stepped in between them, warning Stas, "No one hurts my men."

Stas turned the blade on her, grinning crazily.

"Do *not* touch her," Gavriil growled. "I will never forgive you if you do!"

The tension in the room shot up to dangerous levels as the two brothers faced each other—one with a gun, the other with a blade as they slowly circled each other.

We are all doomed, Rytsar thought.

Wallace stated firmly, "The offer has been made and I stand behind it."

Gavriil turned to him, grateful that there was a way out of the standoff with his brother. "You will act as the worm's payment?"

"Yes," Wallace answered with finality.

Stas walked up to him and nodded to a nearby chair, the mischievous smile growing on his lips.

Wallace sat down as the reality of what was about to happen fell over the room.

Both Captain and Samantha ordered them to stop. In response, several of Koslovs' men subdued the two, forcing them to watch.

Wallace faced the brothers with the same steadfastness Rytsar had when he was a boy facing the whipping pole.

When Wallace turned his head to look at Rytsar with grim resolve while his arms were bound to the chair, Rytsar nodded to him in respect.

Nothing could change the events about to happen, but Rytsar would honor the man's courage by suffering with him. The entire time he kept his gaze locked on Wallace, even as others turned away.

Wallace took it like a man, the way Rytsar would have if the roles had been reversed.

The sickening sound of the eye being popped out, along with the knife cutting into the flesh of the optic nerve and Wallace's cries of agony, filled the room. Watching was far harder for Rytsar than enduring it himself. This was not Wallace's fight and yet he was paying the price—his sacrifice the only way to ensure they all lived.

Rytsar would be forever in Wallace's debt.

Stas held up his prize for everyone to see when he was finished.

The silence in the room was chilling; the only sound was of Wallace's labored breathing.

"It is done," Gavriil announced, finally breaking the silence.

He walked over to Rytsar and looked down at him with disdain. "This is your gift, worm. It will be boxed up and sent to our cousin's family so they may know their son's death has been avenged."

Gavriil then turned to Samantha and smiled as if nothing had happened. "You may leave now. I guarantee your safety, Mistress Clark."

Rytsar took heart hearing his promise to her, because Gavriil was stating to Stas and all the men present that he was back in charge now.

They might have a chance…

"Please deliver the worm to Vlad with our compliments and feel free to play with him before you do." He smirked lustfully at her, adding, "I won't tell."

Samantha rebuffed him, seemingly unamused, and moved over to Rytsar and began untying his bonds, her actions unhurried as if she was unconcerned about their safety, building up Gavriil's ego and feigning her trust.

Captain walked over to Wallace, ripping off his shirt and wadded it up before pressing the material against Wallace's eye socket. He ordered Wallace to hold it there as he quickly made work of the rope.

Once Rytsar was untied, Samantha insisted he turn around so she could bind his hands behind his back. Rytsar hated wasting even a second and did so with great resentment. He was afraid at any moment they might all be shot in the back.

As their party slowly made its way out of the room, Gavriil called out, "Enjoy Hell, Durov, and tell your father hello for me."

Rytsar growled under his breath, already formulating how he would take the *entire* Koslov empire. There was a time when just the brothers' deaths would have sufficed—but not now.

His need for revenge had grown exponentially.

At the door, the three were handed the winter clothing they had entered with. Because he had no shirt, Captain took his jacket but handed Rytsar his fur *ushanka*.

"The head is where we lose most of our heat. Hopefully it will provide you with enough protection."

"It will do," Rytsar replied.

As soon as they exited the building they were hit by a brilliant winter sun and the severe temperatures of a Russian cold front. Having faced the cold in his cell, Rytsar was not shocked by it and smiled at the others, grateful to be alive.

Captain ordered Wallace to lean against him and they

started off. Rytsar was actually surprised when the four of them made it to the outskirts of the Koslov compound unharrassed. He was deeply impressed that the deal Thane had struck through his brother Vlad had been enticing enough to convince the Koslovs to let him go. Rytsar was both curious and terrified to find out what had been promised.

Equally impressive were the three people who'd come to his rescue and gotten him out alive.

He glanced at Samantha, understanding that her handling of the situation had given them this chance. It was a terrible burden to be beholden to someone you hated with every part of your being. Still, he respected her efforts in this.

Then there was Captain. Rytsar would never forget the courage he showed when Stas was ready to cut his only eye from him. The man didn't move, willingly accepting his fate without reservation.

And Wallace…

Up until this point he had thought little of the man, deeply offended by his past interactions with Brie. But the Wolf Pup had changed over the years and after the courage he'd shown today, Rytsar had only the highest regard for him now.

Suddenly, a feeling of unease crept over him and he stopped in his tracks.

"I cannot go yet."

The three looked at Rytsar as if he were crazy, but he ignored them, turning back toward the compound and whistling as loud as he could.

"Are you mad?" Samantha exclaimed.

Rytsar shook his head, looking to the trees, hoping to see movement. He had no idea if the dog was around, but he did not want to abandon it. He wouldn't be here now if it hadn't been for the diligence of the stray.

Rytsar whistled again and started moving back toward the compound, causing his companions great anxiety.

"We are not here to seek revenge today," Captain stated in no uncertain terms.

To Rytsar's relief he saw the dog break through the trees, making a beeline for him. Rytsar forgot his pain as he ran toward the animal, his arms outstretched.

The beast leaped into the air and landed in his arms, whining joyfully as it licked his face.

"What the hell?" Samantha cried, familiar with Rytsar's aversion to animals.

Rytsar turned to face the three, amused by the pink tongue that kept lapping his cheek in gratitude. "This dog helped save my life," he explained. "I could not leave it behind any more than I could a comrade."

"Put it down," Samantha insisted. "You're going to reopen your wounds."

As much as he hated to admit it, Samantha was correct. He could already feel the pain in his ribs intensifying with each passing second. Rytsar let the animal jump out of his arms and accepted Samantha's offer to lean on her as they continued moving forward.

"We can't chance the Koslovs changing their minds," he stated gruffly, wanting her to know that it was the *only* reason he was accepting her support.

"The helicopter is just over the next hill," Captain

informed him.

"I can make that," Rytsar stated. "How about you, Wallace?"

Wallace gave a thumbs-up in answer, unable to speak as he held on to Captain with a white-knuckle grip.

The next hill seemed to take forever to crest, but Rytsar was greatly relieved when they did and he looked back to see that no one was following them.

When he turned back, however, he noticed that the shirt Wallace was holding against his eye was soaked with blood. "Press harder," Rytsar advised him. "You must get the bleeding to stop."

Wallace pushed his palm against the material, grimacing in pain.

Rytsar grimaced with him, hating that he was suffering. Another casualty in a long line of people who knew him.

As they approached the helicopter, Rytsar recognized the face of a person sitting beside the pilot.

"Andrev?" he murmured, snarling under his breath.

Captain spoke up. "Sir Davis had to fight hard after your brothers refused to help."

"Why am I not surprised to hear that about my brothers?" Rytsar spat. "They are worthless men."

"However," Captain continued, "as you can see by your brother's presence, Sir Davis did not take no for an answer."

Rytsar continued to stare at Andrev as they drew nearer. He was extremely displeased to see his brother there. Theirs was a bad history. In fact, he despised his brother, unable to forgive Andrev for his cowardly betrayal years ago. "I wish he hadn't come," Rytsar growled.

Samantha surprised him when she said, "He was the one who convinced the others. Like him or not, you are alive because of Andrev's influence."

Rytsar glared at her. "I have several people I do not care to be beholden to."

Samantha met his disdain without flinching. "I don't expect your gratitude or your forgiveness. I came here because I did not want you to die."

Rytsar frowned. How terrible was fate to make an abusive woman and a treacherous brother be his rescue team?

Glupyy began growling when they got within a few feet of Andrev. Even the dog did not like the spineless cretin.

His brother raised his gun and pointed it at the beast. "Would you like me to shoot the rabid animal?"

Rytsar grabbed his wrist, forcing the gun down. "No one touches my dog." He whistled and pointed. The dog jumped into the helicopter exactly where Rytsar had indicated and sat, waiting.

Captain helped Wallace into the helicopter before boosting Samantha up and climbing in himself.

As the helicopter took off, Andrev turned around and stared at Rytsar, wearing an irritating smirk. "You know what they say about animal *lovers*…"

"My dog would bite your dick off if you tried," Rytsar answered. Deciding to change the name of his venerated pup, he added, "*Mudryy* doesn't suffer idiots."

Andrev scoffed. "Who names a *sobaka* 'wise'?"

Rytsar lifted his chin smugly. "I do. This dog obviously despises you, which only illustrates the canine's superior intelligence."

Andrev huffed and turned around as the helicopter changed direction and started toward Moscow.

Rytsar looked out the window at the disappearing buildings of the compound. He noted the position of them from above, adding it to his knowledge of it from the ground. He suspected the Koslovs would return to Moscow now that he was gone, which worked in perfectly with his plan.

First, he needed to make a few modifications within the compound itself. Then he planned to apply pressure on the Koslov organization. Just enough to send the brothers running back to their isolated compound.

Then the games would begin. Revenge so sweet—on Rytsar's terms.

How profoundly ironic that in trying to subdue their competition through violence and fear, the Koslov brothers had constructed their own demise.

Rytsar turned his attention onto his three rescuers, scolding them. "You should never have done this. The risk was too great—and the cost."

He looked at Wallace with growing concern.

Wallace stated through gritted teeth, "It was my choice, and I would do it again."

The dog seemed sensitive to his pain and whined, thrusting its nose on Wallace's lap and looking up at him in compassion.

Rytsar was moved by the man's uncompromising courage. "I promise I will see to it your sacrifice is not wasted."

Wallace lifted his head. "Yes."

As soon as Samantha saw his worsening condition, she barked a question at the pilot, who pointed to the first aid box. Grabbing it, she ripped through the box, gathering bandages, gauze, saline, antiseptic and gloves.

With care, she removed the shirt from Wallace's face.

The bleeding eye socket was quickly washed out, covered with gauze, and carefully bandaged up. "This only acts as a temporary solution," she apologized. "You are losing blood."

Wallace nodded, applying pressure to the bandage.

Her voice wavered as she told him, "I'm sorry."

"For what?" he asked hoarsely.

Her reply was tinged with remorse. "I wish I could have stopped them."

Wallace shook his head. "None of us would be alive if you had tried. There is no room for regret."

Captain spoke up, obviously upset. "I should have been the one. I have so few years left."

"No," Wallace answered him firmly. "Age has nothing to do with this."

Andrev huffed. "I would *not* have given you my eye, brother."

"No, you wouldn't," Rytsar snarled. "You are too much of a sniveling coward to understand what sacrifice is."

"Not so."

Rytsar glared at him. "I know differently."

"Do you not question why I am here, Anton?"

"Yes, and I am angered by it."

He leaned toward him and said earnestly, "I came to save your life, brother."

Rytsar snarled. "I remember how it ended between us. Your actions proved then that you are *not* my brother."

"I was wrong to have done what I did."

"Wrong?" Rytsar growled. "You betrayed me! There can be no forgiveness after such treason."

"I knew this would be your reaction," Andrev growled. "Nothing I do will change your hatred for me. Yet…I came."

"Only because my true brother forced you," Rytsar countered.

"It is true that the American forced my hand."

Rytsar snorted in disgust.

"But in the end, it was *I* who chose to help. Without me, you would have died."

"Better to die than to be indebted to you."

"You are a fool, Anton," he spat, turning to face forward again.

"I remember well how you begged and pleaded for my help, Andrev. Despite your incredibly long history of spinelessness, I came to your aid because you were my brother. As a Durov, I could not stand by and see you destroyed. Like a *glupyy*, I believed blood meant something. But no. You turned around and immediately stabbed me in the back like the snake you are and have always been."

Rytsar leaned forward and hissed. "I was a fool then, but I'm *not* one now."

He leaned back in his seat and glanced at Wallace,

who had proven to be more of a brother than his own kin. "It is imperative we get him to the hospital."

"You are both headed there," Captain informed him.

Rytsar snarled in disapproval. "I have too much to do and no time."

Captain clamped his hand on Rytsar's shoulder and squeezed until the pain demanded his attention. "You will take care of this body or it will undermine us when we mount the attack."

Rytsar stared hard at the experienced military leader for several moments, then smiled, appreciating his advice and offer. "Agreed."

Captain addressed Samantha next. "Wallace and you will stay behind of course."

"Oh no, I won't," she snapped. "I'm every bit as capable as you are."

"But—"

"Don't give me any sexist bullshit."

"I wasn't going to," he admonished. "Wallace needs someone beside him after the serious trauma he endured."

"Don't use my injury as an excuse," Wallace stated, his blue eye locked on Captain's. "I plan to join you."

Captain pulled no punches, responding, "You are compromised. Not only physically but mentally. Right now you're in shock and can't appreciate the seriousness of it."

Before Wallace could argue Rytsar spoke up, telling him, "I need you to return to America to speak with Thane and Brie. They will have many questions only someone who was there can answer. I also need you back in the States to ensure nothing happens with Lilly."

"But I—" Wallace began to protest.

Rytsar raised his hand to stop any more argument. "You know how I feel about the beast, so I *need* you handling that situation personally. I can't have any distractions if I am to succeed." Although Rytsar's true motivation was to get Wallace safely out of Russia, all his points were valid and did not undermine Wallace's authority.

He watched Wallace struggle with his request. It was admirable that the man wanted to fight alongside him, but it was not wise and Rytsar could not handle any more blood on his hands.

Wallace looked to Samantha, seeking support.

"I agree with Durov," she responded. "You are needed back in LA and you require time to heal."

"I concur," Captain stated firmly.

Wallace looked down at the dog, still resting its head on his lap. With a sigh of resignation, he accepted his dismissal.

Rytsar patted the dog's hind end and smiled at the man. "Good."

Asking for Andrev's cell phone, Rytsar made a phone call to his trusted sub, Dessa. Even though they had been released, it was imperative that they disappear once they reached Moscow.

The Koslovs could not be trusted.

When they landed, her car was waiting for them. Rytsar personally helped Wallace into the car himself, telling Dessa, "Take us to Dr. Petrov, and drive as fast as you can."

"Oh my God, Rytsar," the woman cried when her gaze landed on him. "You're hurt."

He had forgotten how he must look to others who didn't know he'd been imprisoned and tortured for weeks. Rytsar shrugged off her concern with a smile. "It's nothing. But we need to get to Petrov as soon as possible."

Dessa had tears in her eyes as she nodded in answer. "Of course."

Getting such a reaction from her was a surprise to him. Dessa was normally impassive and quiet. Just how bad did he look?

The ride was a silent one. Rytsar petted the dog that lay on his lap, quelling his concern for Wallace's injury, which continued to bleed profusely.

He will be okay, Rytsar assured himself. *He has to be.*

Lesson in Sadism

Rytsar shattered the prolonged silence to distract himself from his growing apprehension by asking, "Why did you really come, Samantha?"

She didn't answer him, so he turned to face her.

Samantha gave him a look of sympathy, saying nothing as she stared at the wounds covering his face and chest.

Rytsar did not appreciate her compassion and growled menacingly.

"Samantha was the only one of us, besides Thane, who knew Russian," Captain explained. "She has played a vital role in the negotiations and your extraction."

Rytsar faced her again. "You spoke to all of my brothers?" he asked with a tinge of disgust.

"Yes."

His familial ties had shattered after their mother was murdered.

"Thane contacted them first, of course," Samantha added.

Rytsar glared at Andrev. He clearly saw the faces of

all four siblings when looking at him, since the Durov men had very distinctive facial characteristics.

Naturally, Rytsar was the best looking of the group, but there were enough similarities to leave no doubt they were brothers. How he wished that was not the case.

He despised the fact they all looked like his father.

In making Rytsar the whipping boy, Vladimir had created an odd dynamic between him and his brothers. They ended up resenting Rytsar as they grew into adulthood because they knew the heavy price he'd paid on their behalf, and had no way to repay it. Rather than feeling gratitude, they'd separated themselves from him.

His father, on the other hand, had taken Rytsar under his wing after abusing him all those years. He was proud to have a son who was strong and unafraid.

Rytsar was introduced to Vladimir's secret BDSM society at the age of fifteen. Rytsar never trusted his father, but he soaked up everything the man taught him because they shared a passion for delivering pain.

The difference between them came in the reason why they enjoyed it.

His father was a weakling inside. His tough exterior hid the truth from everyone. The crueler he became, the more respect he was given until he began to believe he was a great man.

Rytsar was nothing like his father—even though an outsider might disagree. Although they shared sadistic tendencies, Rytsar's sadism was of a purely sexual nature. It turned him on to deliver pain to those who enjoyed it. He savored the unusual power exchange.

Even at the tender age of fifteen, he'd fed off the

energy that pain delivered as pleasure caused. A woman's screams thrilled him and her tears were an aphrodisiac.

He had a voracious appetite for both.

His father took pride in that and pushed Rytsar by offering different scenarios for his son to explore in the kinky and forbidden underground world he'd created.

"How old is she?" Rytsar asked, looking at the naked woman through the one-way glass that separated them.

"Barely legal, son."

"How much experience?"

"One boyfriend."

"Why is she here?"

His father laughed. "She wants to taste the hand of a sadist and is hungry to know the excitement of a man skilled in producing pain."

Rytsar looked at the camera equipment in the room. "Why is it being recorded?"

"She needed the money and was open to the offer."

"Why don't you scene with her then?" he stated, not caring to be filmed.

Vladimir stared at him with a look that made Rytsar's skin crawl. "It's time to critique your growth, son."

Rytsar looked at the naked girl, watching her erect nipples move up and down rapidly as she took shallow breaths. They indicated both her excitement—and fear. He couldn't deny that her need called out to him.

Besides, the girl didn't deserve Vladimir.

"You'll do it then?" his father asked.

Rytsar looked him in the eye, hiding his smile. "I will, but you must leave."

His father furrowed his brow, surprised by the request. "But this task is a critique."

"I understand and you can critique the scene from the video, but I will not scene with her if you are here."

Rytsar relished the disappointment and sexual frustration that flashed across his father's face. He felt a surge of power from it.

After everything Rytsar had been through as a child, there was a deep sense of satisfaction in thwarting his father's will now.

The man was feared throughout Moscow for his ruthlessness and was used to having his own way, so Rytsar took particular enjoyment in pushing his buttons and was clever enough to force his father's hand without consequence to himself.

Vladimir was proud of the prestige Rytsar had gained in the underground community. Since the old man took credit for his son's success and touted it publicly, it gave Rytsar leverage to use against him in times like this.

Rytsar took pleasure in watching his father's face as he realized he faced humiliation if Rytsar refused the lesson after Vladimir had made such a big production of it among his peers.

Needing to keep up the pretense he was in control in front of the others in attendance, Vladimir had to accept that he would not be observing the scene in person.

"I want that video the minute you're done," his father ordered. "I will be thorough in my clinical analysis of it."

"Of course. It will be sent to you directly."

Grabbing his wrist and squeezing hard, Vladimir told him, "No, you will deliver it to me personally and we will watch it together so you can receive my honest critique, *son.*"

Rytsar answered with a curt bow. "Fine."

While his father had saved face in front of his fellow Dominants, Rytsar was the clear victor. Now he was free to scene with the girl—without his father's unwanted interference.

"The other men will be joining you in the room," his father stated, asserting his authority over the scene.

"Naturally," Rytsar answered dismissively. He knew the other Dominants would only act as observers during the live scene. He was accustomed to such attention.

Rytsar watched his father leave abruptly, while the others entered the room and took their respective places around the girl.

This was the first time Rytsar would scene in front of a camera. There was an excitement to that, knowing that this encounter would be preserved.

He planned to teach the girl and anyone who watched how hard a female could come while screaming in pain.

Rytsar walked into the room with a smirk on his face. He looked at the naked girl on the bed, her arms and legs spread wide and bound to the metal frame. She was clearly frightened as she glanced at the intimidating men surrounding her.

The camera operator turned on the lights and suddenly Rytsar could distinguish every detail of the girl, from the goosebumps on her skin to the dark hairs of her inviting mound.

"Get a razor," Rytsar stated to an assistant as he approached the bed.

The girl's eyes grew wide as she watched one of the men leave to retrieve the item.

Rytsar told the girl, "I want to see all of you when we fuck."

She lowered her eyes and bit her lip, but he didn't miss her pleased expression as she nodded in compliance.

In his father's BDSM community, eye contact from a sub was considered a sign of disrespect. It allowed the Doms to keep it an impersonal exchange. It gave them complete freedom during the scene because the submissive was not the focus. She was simply an object of pleasure to be used in any capacity the Dominant desired.

In the case of a sadist, this could prove extremely challenging for a submissive thought of only as an object. Elements such as safewords and aftercare were *not* a part of the experience.

Unlike his father, part of Rytsar's enjoyment came from the release the masochist gained though his delivery of pain. It set his father and him apart, although a casual observer might not notice the difference.

Rytsar demanded a woman who offered herself to him and surrendered completely to his dark desires, but he was conscious of the fact she was a human being, not an object. While he might not care about creating emotional bonds with her, he did secretly crave her enjoyment of the session.

It probably explained why he was so popular among the submissives in their underground community.

When the assistant returned with the razor, Rytsar settled between her legs spread wide and began the intimate task of shaving her. He felt the heat of the lights around him, and heard the camera man move about, even hearing the subtle movements of the Doms observing. He blocked them all out, his only mission to introduce this young woman to his sadistic needs.

Rytsar could feel her thighs tremble as the razor glided over her sensitive pubic area. He smiled to himself as her pussy was made bare, exposing the innocent pink shading under the dark, curly hair.

"That's much better," he stated afterward, wiping her mound with a cloth when he was done. He gently fingered the folds of her pussy, admiring the new territory he was about to lay violent claim to.

The young woman had only been fucked by a boy—now she would be taught the meaning of possession, where his pleasure meant her delicious pain.

Rytsar untied her legs and pushed them up, spreading her ass cheeks apart to stare at the tight rosette. "Have you been fucked in the ass?"

"No…" she gasped, her body tensing.

"You will be today."

He leaned down, kissing the soft outer skin of that forbidden fruit as his lingering promise to her.

Unbeknownst to the girl, he was a full two years younger than she was. However, no one would suspect because he was not only mature for his age, but he knew exactly what he wanted from a woman and possessed the confidence to get it.

He was already formulating in his mind how this scene would play out.

Rytsar never felt intimidated working in front of older, more experienced Doms because he relied solely on his masculine instincts and honored his sexual needs.

He could read a woman and interpret her actions better than most Dominants, but what made him unique for his age was that he knew himself very well. Well enough to move through a scene with confidence, playing with the woman's body and psyche until she embraced the erotic agony he ached to give her.

Rytsar knew, without a doubt, this girl would soon be coming hard around his cock as her screams filled the small room.

It was his gift.

Few men acted on their darkest desires, but Rytsar had no such filters, embracing them all without shame.

Some women were made for it, others could be trained. And then there were those who would run after their first time. He could never know for certain until play began and he was able to gauge her responses.

However, he was certain this session would prove stimulating for them both.

Rytsar untied her wrists, telling the sub, "Restraints are unnecessary because I want you to willingly submit to my pain."

It was an aspect of sadism he found particularly provocative. Convincing a woman to offer herself physically, despite her fear of the pain that was coming.

When the young woman looked up at him, he became entranced. No one mattered in the world except this girl he was about to dominate.

Rytsar lay down on top of her, still fully clothed. He pressed his lips on her throat and bit down. It was an easy way to state his dominance and encourage her surrender. He'd noted it was an instinctual response that seemed common in most predatory mammals.

The girl cried out in surprise and tensed at first, but as he bit down with more pressure he felt her body begin to relax…

Rytsar sought out her lips next, kissing her once before he thrust his tongue in her mouth. He traced her teeth with his tongue and groaned as he plundered her luscious mouth.

It was clear she was inexperienced by the tense way she held her lips, but she instinctively wrapped her arms around him and moaned in pleasure as she gave in to his deepening kisses. If he were to scene with her again, he could teach her how to properly kiss, but for now he took pleasure in her naïveté.

Rytsar pulled away, propping himself up on his forearms so he could look at her. She was a stunning brunette with green eyes. There were hints of his mother in the girl's facial structure, no doubt his father's preferences coming though in the choice of the girl. But her eyes were wider and her lips plumper.

They were lips that begged to be kissed, but he wanted more…

Rytsar began lightly nipping her with his teeth as he explored her body, starting with her sensitive earlobes and traveling down to her jaw. She stilled under him, her breath coming in rapid gasps.

Rytsar took his time, biting harder in more sensitive areas and enjoying her whimpers of pain. He had her completely enraptured when he started toward her mound.

"Oh, *bozhe moy*!" she cried, putting her hand on his shaven head to stop him.

"Hand on the rails," he commanded.

She made whimpering sounds as she reached up and grabbed two of the slats of the metal headboard.

The girl looked so vulnerable lying there, her legs wide open, her head turned out of respect, but her eyes darting every now and then trying to catch a glimpse of what he would do.

Her breathing increased dramatically.

He smiled to himself. This was where his instinctual knowledge of women came into play. Since she was not allowed to see what he was doing, it naturally increased her libido—and fear.

Rytsar lowered his face over her pussy and took a bite of the skin of her outer lip, tugging on it as he pulled away, his teeth grazing her skin.

The submissive grasped the rails tightly, crying out as her legs tried to close to protect her.

"Keep your legs open. Do not move."

The sub closed her eyes as she forced her legs back, struggling with the need to obey him, but knowing he would bite her again.

Those were the moments he cherished. That reluctant but willing surrender to his need.

"Good…" he purred as he leaned down again.

He took the soft fold of her pussy into his mouth, the smoothness of her freshly shaved cunt turning him on as he bit down on the sensitive flesh, his cheek barely brushing against her clit.

Every action, every touch, was thoughtful and meant to arouse through pleasure, fear or pain.

First the pleasure…

The girl shuddered under him as he brushed against her clit a second time before pulling on the flesh of her outer lips with his teeth. She cried out and then moaned when his mouth encased her clit and he began sucking and licking it, teasing that receptive little button of pleasure.

Then he added the pain…

Pulling back on the hood, Rytsar exposed her vulnerable clit. He growled hungrily as he flicked it with his tongue, knowing it was far too sensitive and unused to such direct stimulation. The girl squirmed underneath him, and he reminded her to be still. Pulling the hood back farther, he began sucking hard, interspersing the heavy pressure of sucking with relentless tongue action.

To add to her delicious suffering, he reached up one hand and began playing with her nipple. A simple roll between his fingers to begin before he began to pinch and pull on it.

The girl screamed, the focused attention being far too much for her inexperienced body to handle, and yet he continued, having to put one hand on her stomach to keep her from moving as he continued to torment her clit with his mouth.

When he had her thoroughly wound up, he stopped and lifted himself up to kiss her mouth, his lips covered in her feminine juices.

And then he added the element of fear…

He growled lustfully as he bruised her lips with his kisses. The girl responded well, opening her mouth to invite his demanding tongue.

Rytsar gripped her waist, grinding his hard-on against her pussy as he told her, "I wonder how your pussy would handle it if I used clamps to spread you apart."

She let out a frightened cry, knowing she was not in control of the scene, but soon returned his passionate kisses as he continued seducing her with sexual nibbles and insistent kisses as she mentally accepted her fate and gave in to his desire.

"Before I spread you open I must fuck you."

Rytsar reached down, releasing his hard shaft from his leathers and rubbing it against her overstimulated clit. She'd kept her gaze from him as she should, but he wanted to see her expression when he breached her cunt the first time.

"Look at me."

When her gaze met his, he thrust his cock into her forcefully. The girl cried out, glancing down to see his hard shaft filling her pussy. She looked back up at him in lustful amazement.

He growled huskily. "Erotic, isn't it?"

Rytsar's eyes flashed as he took a tighter hold and showed her just how a man fucked a woman. Her pussy, raw from his previous attention, could not resist him. She threw her head back and screamed as he began pounding her. The moment he stopped, the muscles inside her wet cunt tensed around his shaft and milked him with rhythmic pulses as she came hard around him.

Her Voice

While driving to the doctor, Rytsar made a second call. One he'd dreamed about making ever since his capture.

His hands actually shook after he dialed the number, and was waiting for the other end to pick up. The moment he heard his brother's familiar voice, Rytsar could finally really breathe again. "Brother!"

There was a long pause before Thane answered. "Durov, is that really you?"

In the background Rytsar could hear Brie cry out, "Is that Rytsar, Sir?"

Rytsar smiled, not quiet believing he was back among the living again. He had to keep back the tears because of the other people in the car, although the flood of relief he felt was overwhelming for him.

He affirmed their question, grateful to be alive. "It is I, brother."

Thane's voice faltered, clearly as emotional as he. "Oh hell…I cannot tell you how good it is to hear your voice again."

"I feel the same, comrade."

"Where are you now, my old friend?"

Rytsar heard Brie cry in the background. "He's alive. Oh my God, Rytsar's alive!"

It made him smile to hear her, but they were still in a grievous situation. "Wallace has been injured. We are headed to my physician as we speak."

"How bad is he?" Thane asked somberly.

"It is bad," he said, looking at Wallace. "But…he will live."

"Thank God. And you?"

"I will recover as well, comrade."

Thane attempted to relay the news to Brie but she was crazy with excitement and took control of the phone, crying, "Come home to us!"

Those words filled his heart with deep warmth and he couldn't stop the tear that ran down his cheek. "I will, *radost moya*. Soon."

Thane took back the phone, telling Rytsar with regret in his voice, "I would be there if I could."

"And I would have kicked your ass if you had come. You have Brie and the babe to look after."

Thane chuckled sadly, but Rytsar heard the tension behind it. "What do you need me to do? I feel so helpless here."

"Nothing more, comrade. You have orchestrated a miracle." Rytsar glanced at Andrev. "One I never imagined was possible. What I need you to do now is to explain to *radost moya* that I will come as soon as I can. There are a few things that must be done before my return."

"She needs to hear that from you," Thane replied, and Rytsar heard Thane hand the phone over to her.

Rytsar closed his eyes and Brie sobbed into the phone, "I'm just so happy to hear your voice again." Her voice choked when she added, "I didn't know if I would."

He swallowed down the lump growing in his throat. "*Radost moya*, I need you to be patient with me. I cannot leave my motherland until I have taken care of this new threat."

"Why do your words fill me with dread?" Brie whimpered.

"Did I not promise *moye solntse* a dance?" he reminded her gently.

"You did," she answered, trying to stifle her tears.

"I will keep that promise to her and to you."

"Please, Rytsar, be careful. I need you to come back," she begged. "I won't be able to rest until I see you again."

"You must rest because of the babe," Rytsar insisted.

"Yes, of course…" she said, weeping. Rytsar heard Brie hand the phone back to Thane.

"I need you to be safe, old friend," Thane told him. "Do not take any unnecessary risks."

Rytsar's gaze landed on Captain. "The people you have sent will see to it every move is calculated and well planned out. You do not need to worry."

"I cannot bear it if you wind up back in the hands of the Koslov brothers. They are an unpredictable foe, brother," Thane warned him.

It was obvious he knew exactly what Rytsar planned.

"It is the reason I must stay until this situation is resolved."

Thane said nothing on the other end.

Rytsar assured him, "Gavriil and Stas made a mistake keeping me alive for so long. I know their compound and I know the guards' routines. The attack will be clean but thorough. Soon, the world will be free of their insanity."

"Shouldn't you wait to heal up before you attack?" Thane stated.

"*Nyet.* What they have done to Wallace was gratuitous and cruel. The Koslov organization is no longer stable, brother. Even among the unlawful, there is a set code of conduct. They must be stopped."

"I understand that, but why not regroup and wait for when the time is right?"

"They believe I am going to meet my maker at the hands of my brother, Vlad. There is no better time than now because they won't see it coming."

"Must he be the one to do it?" Brie whimpered to Thane in the background.

"Please explain to *radost moya* that if I do not stop this now, then she, you, and everyone I know will become pawns in their senseless games for power. They are not right in the head and no one is safe unless they are taken out. Besides," he added ruefully, "I have my own need for revenge."

"I understand, brother. But again, the risk seems too great given your current condition and that of Wallace based on what you said."

"Wallace will be returning home. Captain and…"

Rytsar glanced at Samantha, unsure how he felt about her offer to help, but knowing he needed her assistance if he were to pull this off quickly and quietly with as few people involved as possible. "Both Captain and Samantha are staying to assist me."

"How do you feel about that, my friend?" Thane asked, knowing why he had reservations.

Rytsar stared at Samantha when he answered, "I believe we will be able to pull this off and that is all that matters. We cannot fail."

"I am grateful to hear it. Frankly, we could not survive losing you again."

"Agreed," he answered, those annoying emotions coming to the surface again, making him want to cry.

"Hold on a minute, Brie has something that she wishes to tell you."

"Certainly."

Brie got back on the phone. "Rytsar, the baby has grown so much since you left us."

"I'm glad to hear it."

"We were told the sex of the baby at the last appointment. Would you like to know?"

He chuckled. "I already do."

"Yes, you do," she confirmed, "and Sir has come up with the perfect name for her."

"Wait to tell me when I see you both," he said, smiling to himself. "The name of the child is an important thing. I want to hear it from your lips so that I can kiss them afterward."

Brie giggled softly. He could hear the fear behind her every word, but he appreciated that she was trying to cover it up for his sake.

"Send this Russian off with a smile," he told her.

She did not speak for several moments. "I give you my fidelity, protection, and comradeship, Rytsar Durov."

"Ah…that is exactly what I needed."

"I love you," she added.

"And I, you, *radost moya*," he replied. "You fortify my heart."

Thane took the phone back. "When can we expect Wallace to return?"

"I cannot say until my doctor has assessed his situation, but know he will be on the first plane back as soon as possible." Rytsar thought back to Wallace's bravery and said, "He saved us all, comrade. He is a man of honor."

Thane digested his words before replying. "He went in my stead. I look forward to seeing him again, and thanking him myself."

"For the first time, I am glad for your condition. I wouldn't want you here, but I would have been unable to stop you. But know this will be one of the greatest victories no one will ever hear about."

"As long as you come back, my friend."

"Just one more thing," Rytsar said, his eyes darting to Andrev, who had his head turned. "How did you get my brothers to pay the ransom?"

"I simply reminded them who you were."

Rytsar shook his head, unwanted tears welling in his eyes. When he looked back, he saw that Andrev was staring at him. For the first time, in a long time, he saw his brother—not his enemy.

Rytsar watched over Wallace, refusing treatment for himself until Dr. Petrov was able to cauterize the wound and stop the bleeding.

"He will be all right?" Rytsar asked.

"The man will need an infusion, but yes, he will survive." The doctor looked down at his torso with concern. "Now let me examine you."

"Yes, yes," he said dismissively. "But give me a moment alone with him."

"I will be waiting for you in Examination Room four." As he was leaving, Dr. Petrov added, "Don't take long."

Rytsar nodded. He turned to speak to Wallace, who had half of his face now covered in white bandages. "What you did…"

"You would have done as well," Wallace finished.

"But this was not your fight."

Wallace shrugged. "When Davis was organizing the rescue party, I knew I was meant to go."

"Why?" Rytsar asked, needing to know.

"I couldn't imagine a world without your ugly mug in it."

Rytsar burst out laughing, and then cried out in pain because of it. He pointed accusingly at the man for making him laugh, but could not hide his amusement.

Wallace looked him over and said, "I will be okay, Durov. Take care of yourself. You're looking pretty bad."

Rytsar grabbed Wallace's hand and wrapped both of his around it in a show of solidarity. "I am a man who does not forget my debts."

"The only thing you owe me is getting back safely to Brie. Remember, you did charge me with protecting her—and her child."

"I did," Rytsar replied, smiling as he thought of *moye solntse*. He stared at Wallace, recalling the distrust he'd felt when he had been forced to give Wallace the duty due to lack of time.

It felt like a lifetime ago.

"You have done well with my charge," Rytsar complimented, "but before I come home I *must* avenge what the Koslovs did to you, to my mother, and me."

"I get that. Believe me, I do. But don't you let this," Wallace pointed to his bandages, "be for nothing. Make it back alive."

"Of course," Rytsar answered solemnly. "However, I do have one favor to ask."

Wallace responded without hesitation. "What is it?"

"The dog."

He laughed. "You want me to take care of your dog?"

"It cannot come where I am going, and I have grown…attached to it."

Wallace looked at him strangely, seeming thrown off by the respect. "First the cat and now a dog. What's happened to you?"

Rytsar snorted. "They seem to seek me out now. I cannot explain why."

"In any case, I will take your dog. What is its name

again?"

"It has a few names, but for now I am calling it *Mudryy*."

Wallace repeated the word.

"I will be sending you back to America in my private jet. It will make it easier to smuggle the animal aboard," Rytsar said with a chuckle. "However, you must promise to take care of it until my return."

"Is it house-trained?"

"I do not know, but it is a very intelligent animal. I'm sure it would learn fast if it isn't."

"That could be a problem, but I'll get the necessary sundries and accompaniments that go along with owning a puppy."

"Consider it already done. I just needed your permission."

"How long do you expect this to take?" Wallace asked, referring to the attack on the Koslovs.

"It will take time to set up what I have planned, but once ready, it will be like a long line of dominos. One push and it all comes tumbling down." He added with a feeling of elation, "And the best part? We won't even be here when it does."

Rytsar leaned down, telling Wallace in confidence, "No more blood will be spilled on my account. I will see to it."

"Can I give you one piece of advice before you go?"

"Certainly."

"You need to talk it out with Samantha. You do not know how hard she fought and the things she did to save you."

Rytsar growled.

"I understand you have a negative history with her, but take it from me, you can't let it keep eating you inside."

"You have no idea," Rytsar stated angrily. "What happened cannot be forgiven."

"I believe you, but you need to find a way to let it go—for your own sake."

Rytsar eyed him suspiciously. "I am not sure I like this new side of you. When did you become a sage?"

Wallace smiled sadly. "I only speak from experience."

Vodka Shot

Rytsar was held up in a private room for three days while nurses secretly attended to him and Dr. Petrov ran multiple tests.

Everyone gathered in the room when the doctor said he was ready to make an assessment of his recovery.

"According to the tests, you suffered internal bleeding although you've recovered from it. However, you still have internal bruising to contend with, as well as several broken ribs, not to mention the external wounds on your body and face… Basically, you need more time to heal."

"Time is something I do not have. Give me compression bandages to help with the pain and I can leave."

"That is exactly what you *don't* need, Durov. Your lungs are damaged and require time to heal or you risk them collapsing."

Captain, who was standing beside the doctor, said, "I commit to looking after him and making sure he takes off the compression bandages at night so his lungs have a chance to expand. But I am in agreement with Durov. It is time we leave."

Petrov was irritated by their defiance. "Ignore your doctor's orders then. I don't even know why you bothered to ask me."

Rytsar put his hand on Petrov's shoulder. "You have given me a fighting chance by stitching me up and giving me those blood transfusions. Thank you. There is no one else I trust with my health and that of Wallace. You have been invaluable to us."

Petrov sighed in resignation, knowing his advice was being thrown aside. "You are a good man, Durov, but a lousy patient."

Rytsar had to hold back his laughter or risk pain. "Expect a substantial gift to show my gratitude," he stated.

Petrov shook his head. "*Nyet.* This is my payment for what you did for Zhirov's family. We are all beholden to you for finding her and bringing her back home."

"Every girl who is safely returned to her family's arms honors Tatianna's memory. I need nothing more."

"Still, I will not accept any gift from you."

Rytsar was offended and looked him in the eyes. Normally, he would not stomach owing another, but he realized the doctor did not mean the refusal as an offense, so he reluctantly accepted the doctor's gift.

"If you believe in a heaven, then you have gained a gold star, Doctor," Rytsar said with a smirk.

"If I have one, then your heaven must be filled with them."

Rytsar snorted. "We both know where I will be headed. No amount of good deeds makes up for the bad we have done, even if the recipients deserved exactly what they got. It is the price I pay, but I do it willingly so others do not have to."

"I disagree," Petrov stated. "The good you have done for countless families will be rewarded."

Rytsar rolled his eyes. "Maybe. It is possible I will get the luxury suite in Hell."

Petrov chuckled. "I'm sure it would be an interesting place to gather."

"So you will get me the necessary bandages so that I might leave?"

"I do it under duress," he stated, nodding to one of the nurses to get the needed items. "I wish you success in your endeavors and that I never see you again because you have no need of me."

"I hope the same, Petrov," Rytsar agreed.

They left in the dead of night after hearing rumors that the Koslov brothers had men snooping around different parts of Moscow looking for Samantha. Apparently, Gavriil was hoping to score big with the Mistress.

Rytsar had already arranged for Wallace's flight.

Captain, Samantha, and Rytsar walked him onto the plane to see him off.

"Although there will be some initial adjustment," Captain told him, tapping on his own eye patch, "you will be fine, son. We'll talk more when I return."

Wallace nodded.

"And as for your sacrifice, we will honor it with a

resounding victory."

"I know you will," Wallace replied, "and I'll make sure to tell Candy that you will be home soon."

Captain nodded curtly, but his voice gave away his underlying emotion when he said, "Thank you."

Samantha said her good-byes next. "I have no words to express my gratitude for what you've done. We've known each other for several years since living in Denver, but you are now… If you should need anything, I will always be at your disposal. I mean it."

"Thank you, Samantha," he told her. "But let me say this, in case you wake up some night and feel remorse or guilt for how our mission went down. I have no regrets. What happened was my choice and my choice alone."

Rytsar was surprised to see Samantha tear up as she moved away.

Now it was his turn to say his good-byes, but Wallace stopped him. "You've already said your piece, so let me say mine."

Rytsar huffed. "Very well."

"I admire you, Rytsar Durov. I've never met a man with more passion. You live your life upfront and loud, with no pretenses. You are a force to be reckoned with, but everything you do is from the heart. I hope fate continues to cross our paths, because I am a better man for it."

"Enough!" Rytsar commanded gruffly, embarrassed by the praise.

Before anyone noticed the blush on his cheeks, Rytsar dropped down on one knee, and the dog jumped up on him, licking his face.

"I am going to miss you, *Mudryy*," he confessed, surprised at his attachment to the animal.

The dog nuzzled its nose in his chest, wagging its tail wildly.

"I promise to take good care of your pup," Wallace assured him.

Rytsar reluctantly stood up and spoke to the pilot. "Have a telegram sent as soon as you touch down."

"Where to, Rytsar?" he asked.

"Send it to Titov's."

"*Da*, Rytsar. It will be done."

Rytsar gave Wallace one last handshake. When he did so, Wallace pulled him close and whispered, "Talk to her."

He frowned, but nodded, petting the dog on the head before heading down the steps. He heard the dog behind him and turned around, commanding, "Stay."

The dog immediately sat down on its haunches and wagged its tail, but as soon as he turned back around, the dog came up behind him.

"Stay!" he barked more firmly.

The dog sat down again, but it was obvious it was not planning on staying behind in the plane.

Captain grabbed the dog's collar and guided it to Wallace, who took hold of the leather collar. "It'll be fine," Wallace assured him.

Rytsar nodded his thanks and headed out of the plane.

The dog started crying piteously, knowing it was being left behind. The sound of its cries tore at Rytsar's heart. It was embarrassing to feel so deeply for an animal and yet he did. He almost turned around, wanting to comfort it, but Captain came up behind him.

"Animals can't understand what's happening, but it will be fine. In a few minutes, it will have forgotten this unhappy parting and be wagging its tail like before."

Rytsar looked up at the entrance of the plane where the dog's continued cries were emanating.

He wasn't so sure Captain was right, but he did know there was no place for the animal where they were headed. LA with Wallace was the safest place for it. Rytsar called out, "Be a good dog."

At the sound of his voice the dog instantly quieted, but when he did not return up the stairs, it started up again.

Feeling like an idiot, especially in front of a wizened military man, Rytsar added, "I will come back for you, *Mudryy*."

He walked briskly to the car, telling Dessa as he got in, "Let's get out of here. It's time to surprise my old friend."

To Rytsar's vexation, Andrev sat on his left and Samantha behind him, while Captain, the man he preferred to sit with, chose to sit up front with Rytsar's sub.

Having digested Wallace's advice to talk, he knew he should probably speak to Andrev, but he'd told too many lies to be trusted, and there was that bitter betrayal hanging between them. Rytsar didn't know if such a deep rift could be mended, and didn't care to risk it.

So they sat in silence the entire drive.

When they reached their destination, Rytsar asked that the others stand behind him as he rang the doorbell and waited.

It was a surreal moment for him; having said his final good-byes to Titov in America, he'd never really expected to see the man again.

A servant answered the door. It seemed Titov was putting the extra money Rytsar had allotted him to good use. It made Rytsar glad as the man deserved to be waited on after all he had done and been through supporting Rytsar all these years.

The man looked at him strangely. "Whom may I say is calling?" he asked formally.

"Tell Titov it is an old ghost from the past."

"I need more, sir. He is a very busy man and not to be trifled with."

Rytsar smirked. "A ghost with a taste for vodka."

The servant gave him a tight-lipped expression as he looked over the people behind Rytsar, his suspicions suddenly raised. "I will inform him there are visitors. Please wait out here."

Rytsar grinned to himself when the man shut the door on him and left them standing there.

"I don't think he trusts you," Andrev stated.

"Why would he? We look like trouble." He glanced over at Captain, who had several noteworthy bruises, and even Samantha, who had gotten the least of the abuse by the Koslovs, still wore a light bruise on her cheek.

The door suddenly swung open and Titov stood before him. Before Rytsar could say a word, Titov had him in a tight embrace. "You're back!"

"I am," Rytsar replied breathlessly, trying to release Titov's embrace as his lungs screamed out in protest.

"But I am worse for wear."

Titov instantly let go and looked at him with concern. It wasn't until then that Titov noticed the others standing behind Rytsar. Titov stared at each one thoughtfully. Looking at Rytsar with a worried expression, he insisted, "Come in." He then extended the invitation to the others. "Come in all of you."

He barked to his servant, "Get them whatever they need. I would like to speak to Rytsar alone."

Titov guided him down the corridor to his parlor. There on the table was the bottle of Zyr and shot glass Titov had promised.

He sat Rytsar down before picking up the bottle and pouring Rytsar a generous amount while he explained, "I have gazed upon this table every day since my return to Russia, praying by some miracle that you would come to claim it."

Handing the full glass over, he confessed to Rytsar, "I was struggling to face the future without your direction."

"You need to pour another. I refuse to drink alone."

Titov grinned, leaving the room to get a glass. He returned quickly with it and another bottle of Zyr. "Just in case," he stated, setting it down.

After pouring his own glass, he held it up and toasted, "To a good man who cheated death."

Rytsar raised his own. "Some bastards cannot die." He gulped down the warm liquid, tears coming to his eyes from the sheer pleasure of it.

Titov immediately poured another before sitting down next to Rytsar and staring at him as if he were truly looking at a ghost.

It made Rytsar uncomfortable. "What's wrong?"

"You look terrible. I almost didn't recognize you when I opened the door."

"I'm sure it's not that bad," Rytsar replied, but he recalled Dessa's reaction when she first saw him.

"No, you really do," Titov insisted, getting up and leaving the room again, returning with a mirror a short time later.

Rytsar looked at his reflection and was shocked by what he saw. His eyes were sunken, his cheeks hollow, one of them covered by a line of a hundred tiny stitches. He was reminded of Frankenstein.

"Well, I guess fate has seen to it that my outside now matches my wretched soul." Rytsar laughed, setting the mirror down.

"At least you escaped! I never imagined you would leave the Koslovs alive."

"Those people out there," he said, nodding toward the door, "they came to my rescue."

Titov looked concerned. "I would have tried but you gave me strict orders."

"And I am grateful you kept your promise. Those people almost died, Titov." Rytsar felt the weight of Wallace's sacrifice on his shoulders. "The Wolf Pup—"

"Did they kill him?" Titov asked in concern.

"No, but after they received the ransom from my brothers, they insisted on a sacrifice that could not come from me. He volunteered and now his suffering has become my suffering."

"Where is he now?"

"On a plane to America. As far away from here as possible."

After downing the second shot, Titov refilled for a third time knowing Rytsar needed it.

"How did your brothers get involved? I was shocked to see Andrev."

Rytsar looked at him ruefully. "My real brother forced them."

Titov nodded.

"Truthfully, I still do not trust Andrev. How can I? Even though I was told he was instrumental in getting Vlad, Timur, and Pavel to step up, I cannot forget our past."

Titov sighed deeply. "Your brothers, they have not lived in reality. I would not trust any of them with my life."

"And yet they were part of my rescue."

"I see Ms. Clark is with you as well," Titov stated offhandedly.

Rytsar growled in anger. "Can you believe I am beholden to that woman as well?"

Titov frowned. "Such an odd band of liberators."

"That's what I think." Rytsar lifted the glass and downed his third shot. He smiled afterward. "I must say, I have missed the welcomed warmth of vodka…"

"I bet you have. Would you like me to get you some food to go with that?"

"Pickles," Rytsar answered with a grin. "I am missing the pickles."

Titov pressed a button on the wall and his servant answered. "We forgot the pickles."

"I'm on it, sir," he replied.

Titov turned to Rytsar with an embarrassed look. "I am still getting used to the servant thing."

Rytsar chuckled. "It was about time, old friend. You have served me long enough."

Titov perked up and stated, "I am going with you."

"Where?" Rytsar questioned, having said nothing of his plans.

"You are going to kill the Koslovs. I will help you."

"Why do you think that?"

"You are Rytsar Durov."

Rytsar leaned over, looking him in the eyes. "You have been by my side through all the difficult tasks. It's time you retire."

Titov shook his head. "*Nyet.* It will do my heart good to vanquish the men who did this to you."

"It is not just the brothers I am after, Titov. I want to take down their entire organization."

"Even better."

The servant arrived with the pickles and set them on the table before leaving. Rytsar poured another shot and clinked it against Titov's. "You were a fool to hook up with me."

After they drank the shots down, Titov suddenly became solemn. "Do you remember your father's last days?"

"Of course," Rytsar stated.

"You granted me the revenge I sought."

"You deserved no less."

"It was important for me… I want you to have that with the Koslov brothers."

"Thank you."

Titov snorted. "Maybe once they are gone we can return to our youthful days and create all kinds of mischief together."

Rytsar smiled, but it soon faded. "Those days were full of good memories, but they always get overshadowed by one."

Titov sighed. "I know."

Both men set down their glasses.

"I still miss her, Rytsar," he admitted.

"Every damn day," he agreed.

Looking at Titov, Rytsar decided to speak what was on his mind. "There's one thing I know."

"What's that?"

"Tatianna would be proud of you. I thought of that while I lay dying and figured I should tell you."

Rytsar was surprised to see tears fall from Titov's eyes as he turned away to face the wall. Titov was not one to cry, having become a severely stoic man after his sister's death.

"I'm sorry if I overstepped," Rytsar apologized.

Titov turned back to him, shaking his head. "*Nyet*..."

Pressing further, he asked, "Have you thought of settling down, Titov? Starting a family of your own? I'm certain Tatianna would have wanted that for you."

"What about you?" Titov scoffed. "Still single after all these years?"

Rytsar tilted his head and smiled. "*Moye solntse* will be here soon and I, her only *dyadya*, get to hold her in my arms and tell her I love her. I feel nothing but joy."

Titov only nodded.

"You should know that kind of joy."

"Maybe..."

"You should," Rytsar encouraged.

"After we take care of the Koslovs, then I will think about it."

Reconciliation

The time had come to take Wallace's advice.

Before they set out to claim the remote compound in Siberia, he needed this strangeness between them settled. Working with people one did not trust would only lead to failure and death.

Rytsar took a deep breath, reminding himself that he was the one who had requested this, when he went to answer the knock.

This is my decision.

He opened the door abruptly, making Samantha jump a little. Without smiling, he gestured her inside.

Samantha had dressed in her traditional tight-fitting business attire and stiletto heels. It was her armor of choice.

"Sit," he instructed, sitting opposite from her across the coffee table.

After several moments of silence, she asked, "You said you wanted to talk?"

"I did."

Rytsar looked her over, assessing her. The woman

still had the same look and overall style that had attracted him when they first met in college; that sleek blond hair, the high cheekbones, arched eyebrows, and that confident aura she oozed. But looking at her now, he noticed the lines of age on her face, the haunted look in her eyes she tried to hide, and the nervous way she pursed her lips.

While Samantha allowed him free rein to look her over, she took advantage and did the same to him. It was disconcerting, considering they hadn't spent any time together alone since…

Since that time he'd tried to choke her to death.

"I do not know where to begin," he finally told her.

"Take as long as you need," she offered.

Rytsar shook his head slowly, finally asking, "Why did you come?"

Samantha frowned. "I told you, I didn't want you to die."

"But why risk your life when you knew how much I loathe you?"

She sat back, staring at him intensely before answering. "I may deserve your hatred, but my feelings for you remain true."

"Hah!" he huffed. "What you did I can never forget."

She shook her head. "I wish I could take it back, all of it back. I have done everything I can think of to earn your forgiveness."

"And you thought this would do it?"

Samantha smiled sadly. "I gave up on forgiveness a while ago. Now I just want to do no harm."

Her answer pricked at his heart.

"Did you never think once how I would feel if you all had died? I didn't need your blood on my hands. I didn't want to be rescued."

She answered simply, "Thane believed he could help get you out alive, and I trusted him."

Rytsar glared at her, remembering the humiliation and pain she'd inflicted on him that one night so long ago. "I loved you once. Maybe not in the romantic sense, but it was real and intense."

Her eyes filled with tears. "I know. I felt the same way."

He shook his head violently. "You did not! You would never have done what you did if you felt the way I did."

"I was drunk, Rytsar, and in blind lust for you. I wanted to impress you by showing what I could do—that I was woman enough to Dominate you."

"Even when I continuously ordered you to stop?"

Tears began streaming down her face. "I can't explain why I needed you to surrender to me."

"It was not a power exchange. It was a violation so deep it almost destroyed me."

"I know…" she cried.

"There was only one reason I did not report it."

She nodded her head slightly, swiping at her tears.

"I wanted to put it so far behind me that I could convince myself it never happened. But you…you couldn't let sleeping dogs lie. No, you kept seeking me out, begging for absolution without any thought to me."

"That's not true," she protested.

"And now you come back all these years later, after we had agreed never to speak again. How do you think that makes me feel?"

She looked at him with sorrow but slowly straightened her back and wiped away her remaining tears. "I cannot undo the past, and I know I have only incurred more of your wrath, but I am *not* sorry you are alive. I'm grateful I was able to help to ensure you made it back to Thane and Brie."

The mention of those two pulled his thoughts into a new direction.

He remembered the hopelessness he felt when the door to his cell had been shut that final time and he'd confronted the reality he was going to die there.

He truly thought all had been lost…

Rytsar's gaze drifted back to Samantha again. The woman in front of him changed his fate. Every moment since he was dragged out of that cell to make the ransom exchange was due in part to Samantha.

He continued to stare at her, wondering if the unforgiveable could be forgiven in the right circumstances.

She swallowed hard under his gaze and finally asked, "Are we done here?"

"*Nyet.*"

The minutes dragged by as he contemplated if he could find it within himself to truly forgive her.

"Do you love Brie?" he finally asked.

She was startled by the question. "What do you mean?"

"Do you love her?"

Samantha smiled uncomfortably. "I have come to

believe she is a good fit for Thane."

"And if he were not in the picture?"

She frowned. "What are you getting at?"

"If you went back to the beginning, before there was a negative history between you and her, tell me, how did you feel toward her?"

"I liked her."

Rytsar raised an eyebrow, not satisfied with that answer.

"Yes, I'll admit, there is something special about Brie. I find it intriguing and my admiration for her had grown since," she replied with a blush.

He then asked his next question. "And Thane, what are your feelings toward him?"

Samantha did not hesitate. "You know how I feel. He has been everything to me. A mentor, a friend, the person I trust most in the world."

"Do you love him?"

"Yes, of course. He's like family to me, except my own family were never as good or as kind as he is."

Rytsar took in what she had said, mulling it around in his mind.

Yes, it was possible…

He stood up and looked down at her, stating, "I grant you forgiveness. I will always despise what you did, but I will no longer hold it against you."

Samantha stared up at him with a stunned look.

"Because of the risk you took, Samantha, I will be returning to those I love most. For that, I would give anything. Therefore, my forgiveness is yours."

Samantha stared at him, her lips trembling.

"Rytsar…I—"

He held up his hand. "Today you and I start a brand-new chapter."

"What…what does that look like?" she asked in the barest of whispers, seemingly afraid this new alliance might break at any moment.

"We will not bring up the past again. You and I will concentrate *only* on the future of Thane and Brie."

Samantha nodded, but added hesitantly, "There is *one* thing I must tell you."

His eyes narrowed, afraid she was going to dredge up the past again when he had specifically ordered her not to. "Does it involve what happened that night?" he asked angrily.

"No. I will never speak of it again, as I promised."

"Very well then. What did you want to tell me?"

"I…" She hesitated, making Rytsar nervous. "I want you to know that Ms. Taylor and I had a relationship—of sorts, once."

"Ms. Taylor?" Rytsar asked in shock, completely blindsided by her confession.

"Yes, I broke it off before the wedding in Italy for personal reasons."

"Why did she not tell me herself?" he demanded.

Samantha smiled sadly. "She was afraid you would turn her away."

"And I would have!"

She paused before saying, "I have heard that Lea was very moved by her encounter with you."

Rytsar growled, feeling deceived by Ms. Taylor. "Why are you telling me this?"

"One, you should know and two, I hoped her association with me would not change your future interactions with her."

"She and I will have to have a talk," he growled.

Samantha nodded.

"Is that all?"

"Yes."

Rytsar walked to the window, his emotions tied up in knots. To forgive Samantha was monumental for him, but to find out she and Ms. Taylor were lovers was a shock.

He wasn't even sure how he felt about the girl.

Still…Samantha had told him about it now, despite the fact it might jeopardize her own situation. He respected her for that.

Rytsar turned around. "I am glad you told me."

She nodded. "You deserved no less."

"And I will remind Ms. Taylor of that when I see her again."

His next order of business was to speak to Andrev, his treacherous brother. He was uncertain how it would go, but again the motivation to do so was strong since Andrev insisted on being a part of the attack.

Although they desperately needed the extra manpower, Rytsar had to be convinced Andrev could be trusted with their lives, and that was a tall order.

"Brother," Andrev said when he walked into the

room.

Rytsar frowned, still bristling when hearing that word come from his mouth. The man who could betray his own sibling as well as turn on him when he told the truth about their mother's death did not have any right to utter that word.

"Sit," Rytsar commanded.

Andrev raised an eyebrow, but sat down where he had indicated. "What is this about?" he asked, looking uncomfortable.

Rytsar went straight to the point. "Why should I ever trust you again?"

Andrev smirked. "I suppose 'because I'm your brother' won't work as an answer."

Rytsar didn't even reply, blinking his eyes slowly.

"Fine. I saved your ass from the Koslovs. That's a major plus."

Rytsar frowned, looking at him distrustfully. "You could be working with one of their rivals now. I wouldn't put it past you."

"You know the Durovs don't do business with the *bratva*!" he spat.

Rytsar remained unconvinced. "Some are certainly spineless enough to start."

Andrev stood up. "Is this just an excuse to insult me, is that what this is?"

"Sit down," Rytsar commanded firmly.

Andrev did, but reluctantly.

"I do not have to be polite or even civil to you. You were the one to betray me, *brother*."

"Are you ever going to let that go?"

Rytsar howled, pointing to the door. "Out!"

Andrev stayed where he was, but he held up his hand apologetically. "Look, I'm sorry. I really am. It's not something that comes easily to me—this whole apology thing." He reached into his pocket as he continued, "I've been waiting a long time to do this."

Rytsar eyed him suspiciously.

Andrev pulled out his wallet and held it out to him. "Here."

"What? You want me to steal from you to make this even?" Rytsar asked in disgust.

"No. It's all there. All of it."

Rytsar stared down at the thick wallet but made no move to take it.

"I knew I couldn't face you without paying you back every cent."

"It was never about the money," Rytsar growled.

Andrev shook the wallet. "It wasn't for you, but it was for me." He met Rytsar's gaze. "I needed to scrape up this money, every last ruble, because I owed you something. You know I'm not a rich man by any means. This took me years, Anton. While I can't change the past, I want you to know I *am* sorry. I have been sorry for a long, long time."

Rytsar's gaze drifted down to the wallet again. "What about your wife and children? You made them suffer for this?"

"My woman has always been in support of my reconciliation with you. In fact, she was the one who suggested it." Andrev held out the wallet farther. "Please, take it."

Rytsar finally reached out and took the worn leather billfold. He had been serious that the money was unimportant to him; however, he opened the wallet and took out the cash for Andrev's sake.

"Count it," Andrev said.

Rytsar looked at him for a moment before slowly counting out the bills. He could imagine the years of sacrifice his family must have gone through to save up this amount. He held the bills in his hand, shaking his head. "Why now?"

"It has weighed heavily on my soul, brother. I knew the only way to lift it was to return what I took from you, even though I cannot undo the circumstances that surrounded it." His voice shook when he continued, "That moment when I was informed you had been captured by the Koslovs and possibly dead, I couldn't fathom it. The idea that you would never know how sorry I am."

Rytsar swallowed down the lump in his throat. "What caused your change of heart? You were very adamant about your hatred toward me."

Andrev looked down at his hands, wringing them together nervously. "I have always admired…and hated you."

"Why?" Rytsar demanded.

"You were the only one of us to ever stand up to Father. All of us were terrified of him and we witnessed what he was capable of whenever he punished you."

"I survived."

"You did, but I always suspected you resented us for it. Those punishments were meant for us, not you. How could you not hate us for it?"

"I took those punishments because Father forced me to. It had nothing to do with you." He narrowed one eye, adding, "However, I would have hoped you'd have held back on misbehaving so much."

"We did. We all tried, at least," Andrev insisted. "We lived in dread of being caught and having to watch you get dragged to the pole."

Rytsar shrugged. "It did not feel that way to me. However, I always saw it as my fight against Father, not with you four. It was his doing."

Andrev looked ashamed. "As I said, I assumed you already hated us. While I could understand Mama doting on you because of his unfair treatment, I could not grasp why both Grandfather and Father favored you so. It was as if the rest of us didn't matter to them. We felt worthless."

Rytsar thought about Andrev's words before speaking. "What Father saw in me was my thirst for sadism, something I shared with him that you four did not."

"But how could he go from beating you unconscious to showing you off to his old cronies like you were his firstborn son, his protégé?"

"I cannot explain the innerworkings of that bastard."

"Okay, here's an even bigger question I have been wondering. Why did you allow it?"

"Allow him to teach me everything he knew about sadism?" Rytsar smiled. "Because I *craved* it, so I used all his knowledge, all his influence and resources to take away as much as I could for my own benefit. It was never about him—it was always about me."

Andrev took in a deep breath and let it out slowly. "I am beginning to understand how very little I knew you."

"No, you did not know me. None of you even tried to know me. I was just your whipping boy. But…" he paused, before adding, "Having years to think back on it, I do not believe Father would have allowed it even if you *had* tried. Keeping us separated was part of his plan. If we had ever come together as one, the Durov brothers would have been a force for him to reckon with."

Andrev smiled to himself, as if he were imagining such a thing. But soon his smile faded and he looked at Rytsar accusingly. "There is something else."

Rytsar said nothing, waiting for the next shoe to fall.

"Why did Grandfather choose you over our father, even over Vlad, the oldest of us siblings, to be the next in line for his inheritance?"

"How do you expect me to answer that?" Rytsar scoffed. "Grandfather didn't even tell me about the inheritance. That decision ended up putting me in great peril when Father decided he would take it from me."

Without permission, tears began to well up in Rytsar's eyes as images of Tatianna and his mother came to his mind.

"But how could Father know and you not?" Andrev insisted.

"Based on what Nikolay Koslov told me, very few people understood the significance of Grandfather's ring. Father was one of them."

Andrev glanced at the ring on Rytsar's finger, and a glint of jealousy shone in his eyes.

"There was a time when I would have gladly given

you this ring and everything that goes with it had you but asked. However, that is no longer true," Rytsar informed him. "I have suffered too many deaths because of it, and it is now my burden to bear—this massive collection of rubles."

"I wish I could have such a burden," Andrev mumbled.

"*Nyet*!" Rytsar snarled. "You would not want the curse of this wealth. Much like the whipping pole, I was chosen to suffer so that you four could live out normal lives." He glared at Andrev. "I have made it my mission to use this money to change lives rather than destroy them."

"You know your own kin could use some of that money."

"What? You?" Rytsar growled, certain this was what Andrev had been getting at the entire time. He threw the money Andrev had given him and watched it fan out before it cascaded to the ground at his brother's feet.

"Not me," Andrev stated, looking hurt as he stared at the money on the floor. "Timur's going blind and needs an operation to save his vision. Pavel has twins on the way, but they only have room and supplies for one."

"I did not know Timur is going blind. And twins…Pavel is having twins?" Rytsar asked, now understanding how deep the rift was that separated them.

"We had no right to come to you with our concerns when we did not even let you come to Mama's funeral."

Pain flashed through Rytsar's eyes. All those old feelings and old resentments came flooding back again, and

Rytsar had to fight hard now to keep them from overwhelming him. "That day, when you defended Father, and told me that you wanted that murderer to stand by *Mamulya's* grave instead of me. That was unforgiveable, Andrev."

"We had no idea at the time!"

"I *told* you."

"I've explained our way of thinking back then. We saw you as an enemy to the family, not its protector."

"I do not know if there is any chance of reconciliation," Rytsar stated coldly.

Andrev knelt down and began collecting the money until he had every single bill back in his hands. He stood up and thrust the money out to him. "Brother, I know I was wrong. I have worked hard for years to prove to you how truly sorry I am. All of us—Vlad, Timur, Pavel, and I—came together as one to rescue you because we understand now."

Rytsar laughed sarcastically. "You only did because my brother, my *real* brother, told you to."

"*Nyet*," Andrev insisted. "Vlad was against negotiating for a ransom when the Koslovs first presented him with their offer, yes. But there were several reasons behind that, and while it's true that your American friend—"

Rytsar quickly corrected him. "My *brother*."

Andrev shrugged but amended himself, "Your American brother."

Rytsar gave him a look of satisfaction, stating, "Continue."

"Your American brother reminded Vlad about the

role you were forced to play as our family's unwilling but effective protector. However, he didn't stop there. Davis also informed us about what you've done since Mama's death. I am honored and proud we carry the same blood."

Rytsar shook his head.

Andrev continued, "So with some pressuring from me, Vlad finally agreed to the ransom and Davis's plan to get you out safely."

"And why were you included in the rescue?" Rytsar asked, knowing Thane would never have suggested it.

"If you remember, Vlad is a stubborn and distrustful soul. Therefore, he insisted I accompany the Americans sent to liberate you." There were actually tears in Andrev's eyes when he confessed, "It was frightening to know how close it was—our failure to save you."

"It's true, I almost died."

More than once…Rytsar thought silently.

Andrev nodded with a look of uneasiness.

"So, what happens next is up to me," Rytsar stated.

"More or less," he replied, staring at the money in Rytsar's hand.

"You have given me this 'offering' as an apology."

Andrev licked his lips. "I have, brother."

"And the four of you hope for reconciliation."

He shook his head. "*Nyet*, we don't expect that."

"But you would wish it?"

He looked at Rytsar hopefully.

Rytsar shook his head, unhappy that he must once again forgive the unforgiveable. Still…Wallace had been correct in saying that there were some things in the past that could hold a person hostage. This history between his brothers was one of those things.

"Andrev," he began formally, "I accept your offering and your help in avenging our mother. In exchange, I will forgive your betrayal."

Andrev began to cry silently in relief.

"I also forgive my brothers for..." His voice broke, the pain of his mother's death and his brothers' unified rejection of him still having the power to overwhelm. "You are all forgiven for keeping me from seeing *Mamulya* laid to rest."

Andrev flinched, the words spoken aloud highlighting the harsh reality they made him bear alone.

With his head hanging down Andrev said quietly, "Thank you, brother."

Rytsar crossed his arms as he looked at him. Although the pain had not lessened, his anger over it was beginning to lose its tight hold.

That was the power behind forgiveness. A profound power only the wielder could release.

Payback

Vlad made a few well-placed comments around those he knew to be informants of the Koslov brothers about the execution of his worthless brother, showing off Rytsar's ring as evidence. His proud claims that he was now in charge of the Durov fortune quickly reached the Koslovs, and they sent him a message of congratulations.

With the Koslovs confident their foe had been vanquished, the heightened security force, including those they had employed in the remote compound to the north, was scaled back.

It made it that much easier when Rytsar and his team came in to claim it.

With Captain's expertise, and Rytsar's personal knowledge of the compound, it had not been difficult to secure the isolated area and take control without anyone being the wiser.

Now, they had the privacy they needed to set up the trap that would ensnare the brothers and those closest to them. With the top echelon dead, the entire Koslov

Empire would be thrown into chaos. With so many groups within the *bratva* vying for power, the leaderless Koslov organization would be ripped to shreds as the various factions snatched up what they could—effectively ending the reign of the once proud empire.

Rytsar's heart beat faster whenever he thought of it. Knowing that the Koslov family was now involved in human trafficking only made their impending demise that much more satisfying to him.

Being a man of humor and dark passions, Rytsar had already planned how each of the brothers would die. Both deserved deaths specially handcrafted for the individual. Although Rytsar would not be there when it all went down, he'd made certain both brothers were made aware of who had brought about their ultimate ruin.

He was finishing the final details at Titov's place, assigning each person their tasks.

"Samantha, you will be assisting Captain in constructing the devices while Titov and Andrev will be charged with procuring whatever supplies are needed."

He faced the two men, adding, "I am counting on you being discreet in your purchases.

"As for me, I will assist wherever I am needed until this mission is complete. Time is of the essence, so rest will be a rare commodity until we are done here."

"Understood," Titov immediately replied.

Captain slapped Rytsar soundly on the back. "It's good we are fighting on the same side. You would have made a dangerous adversary, had we met on the battlefield."

Rytsar inclined his head toward the man. "I feel the same, Captain. I have only the highest respect for your knowledge and ingenuity. I truly believe we will accomplish what we've set out to do without endangering ourselves."

Captain snorted. "If these men did not deserve what was coming, I would actually feel sorry for them—but I would still laugh."

Rytsar smiled wickedly. "I find humor is often overlooked in death. It's a shame."

"But why go to such lengths?" Samantha asked him.

A cold smile spread across Rytsar's face. "I believe in destiny and justice. I want to rob these men of their dignity in death. They need to pay for the death of my mother, and for the torture of Wallace."

Rytsar glanced at Captain and grinned. "I am fortunate to have a man with a mechanical background and a mind for chess. He has already planned out how to separate the brothers from the rest of their men, so they can experience the grand finale." He swept his hands wide and laughed. "It will be a purely automated assassination."

Samantha looked at Captain skeptically, shaking her head.

"You have always been a man of extravagance," Andrev stated. "It appears to be the case even when planning a death of an enemy."

"This seems like madness," Samantha told Captain.

"No, Durov is quite frankly…a genius." He looked at Rytsar with respect. "It is rare that you can deliver the kind of death a man deserves."

"And at such a low risk," Rytsar replied with a smirk. "We'll be on our way to America, watching it unfold on a closed-circuit screen. No witnesses and no evidence to tie us to their deaths."

"How can you be sure?" Samantha asked.

Rytsar's grin grew even wider. "Because the grand finale will end with a giant explosion obliterating the entire place."

Captain explained matter-of-factly, "A military-grade drone will fly over the site, dropping an explosive powerful enough to leave only a crater when the debris clears."

"And you think you can find one of those?"

Titov gave Samantha a modest smile. "I have my connections."

It had taken weeks to construct the traps. Each person proved invaluable as they worked efficiently and without complaint, testing and retesting to make certain every element performed flawlessly.

Once Captain was satisfied, they moved on to phase two.

Information was covertly leaked through *bratva* channels that one of the factions was secretly plotting to overthrow the Koslov Empire. The brilliance was that two different factions were being named through two different channels, causing chaos within the entire criminal organization because neither faction knew who was pointing the finger at them.

Feeling the pressure from all sides, it was only natural the Koslov brothers would escape with their top men to hide in their Siberian compound until the dust settled and targets could be assigned.

With the end in sight, Rytsar announced to his team that this would be their last night together before the group disbanded. While he would head back to America with Captain and Samantha, Andrev would return to his family and Titov would stay in Russia to begin a new life of his own.

"It has been an honor to work with you all," Rytsar told them as they sat around the large round table—the very same table the Koslov officials would gather around just before they died.

"Never before has such a thing been attempted—and by so few men…" He glanced at Samantha, adding, "…and women. We will be making history even though our names will never be associated with it."

"Here's to anonymity," Captain toasted, holding up a glass of water, since vodka had not been part of their rations—per his orders.

"How does it feel, Rytsar, knowing you will be free from looking over your shoulder for retaliation after this?" Samantha asked.

He sighed, lost in thought for a moment. "The Koslov brothers almost accomplished what they set out to do but, thanks to all of you, I sit here today and am about to avenge my mother's death. It will allow me to bring closure to a difficult chapter in my life."

Rytsar furrowed his brow, thinking back on his

mother and her last moments. Justice would finally be his, and the obligation to right that wrong would be over.

It didn't seem real—none of this did.

"I never thought I would be free of so many burdens," Rytsar stated, looking at Samantha first and then at Andrev. "So, with this being our last night together, I brought a gift for you all."

"Not alcohol, I hope," Captain said.

Rytsar laughed. "I respected your wishes, Captain."

He handed each person a small box, explaining, "I am a sentimental Russian." As they opened the gifts, he explained, "Each of you has a watch with an inscription on the back to remember this moment."

Titov read the inscription out loud in Russian the way it had been written.

Samantha translated it, her voice low, "The hour of reckoning is here…"

"Thank you," Captain told him, putting the fine timepiece on his wrist.

Titov looked at the watch and then at Rytsar, saying nothing verbally, but speaking volumes with his gaze.

Rytsar nodded to him. "Your allegiance to me is at an end after tonight, my friend."

Andrev stood up and put his hand on Rytsar's shoulder. "Thank you, brother."

"Go back to your family with my blessing and give your woman a kiss from me."

Rytsar had already arranged to have an eye-specialist contact his brother. The doctor would claim to be looking for people with Timur's unique eye condition who were willing to try a fully funded "experimental" procedure. As far as his brother, Pavel… his young wife was about to become a random sweepstakes winner, the money from which would take care of the extra expenses of twins.

Although Rytsar was not ready to meet with his brothers in person, he needed to know they were all well.

Samantha slipped her watch on and told him solemnly, "I will wear this with pride, Rytsar."

Rytsar was pleased to see her put it on. It would act as a reminder of what she'd done for him here—if or when his old feelings of rage threatened to take over.

As they talked late into the night, it gave Rytsar a chance to learn a little more about Captain. He was an extremely private man, having been treated like an outcast by most of the world because of the physical damage done to his face and body during the war.

But it wasn't the outside scars that defined him.

"You never forget, no matter how much time passes. Each death is a burden I carry."

"How many did you lose that day?" Rytsar asked, understanding the heavy weight of that burden.

"Sixty-two," he answered without flinching. "Sixty-two men who were under my command."

"What happened?" Samantha asked.

"We were supposed to have reinforcements bring up the rear when we were told to take that hill, but the other regiments never showed and we were surrounded. It was a slaughterhouse with no way for me to protect my men, and nowhere to retreat."

"How did you survive?"

Captain closed his eyes, sighing heavily. "My only

goal was to shield as many of them as I could from the gunfire, but then the enemy launched grenades. I was hit and should have died."

He buried his head in his hands, groaning. "I *wish* I had died with my men. Instead, the three of us who survived the bloodbath were split up and taken to separate enemy camps."

He looked up at Rytsar, shaking his head in sorrow. "The other two didn't make it and none of my men received a proper burial. Instead, they were heaped into mass graves and covered up as if they were trash."

A tear ran down his scarred cheek.

"So, something like this," Captain said, looking at each of them. "It gives me solace. While I can't change the past, being able to use my military experience to take down an unstable regime—it means something to a haunted old man."

Samantha reached out, placing her hand on his. "We all suffer from pasts that need reckoning."

Captain nodded with a grim look of agreement.

Rytsar asked Titov to join him outside before the hour grew too late. It was time to part ways, but he found it far more difficult than he'd anticipated.

When Rytsar had said his final goodbyes to Titov in LA, believing he was about to die, it hadn't affected him nearly as much as it was affecting him now.

They'd become inseparable while working together to exact revenge on Vladimir Durov. Afterward, Titov decided to become his right-hand man. Together, they found solace because of the tragic past they shared.

Although Rytsar had moved on, carving out a life for

himself, Titov had been content to stand in the shadows acting as his support. He took pride in Rytsar's accomplishments, and never looked to break away from their comfortable routine.

Now it was time for Titov to move on.

Naturally, Rytsar wanted a rich future for his friend, but the thought of not seeing him on a daily basis was difficult to face. It was like losing a part of himself, a part he had grown to count on.

"Shall we drink to your health?" Rytsar asked, producing a bottle he'd hidden from Captain.

Titov laughed, looking him over. "I think your health would make better sense, since you are in such poor shape."

"Then to your future," Rytsar suggested.

"What little of it I have left."

Rytsar punched him playfully. "Stop with all the negativity." He held up the vodka and made a toast, "To a family that proudly carries on your name."

Titov chuckled. "If I can find a woman who will have me."

"There you go again," Rytsar complained, taking a swing before handing him the bottle. "Now drink up, you depressing bastard."

A feeling of somberness enveloped them both as they drank.

"I can still go with you to America," Titov offered.

Rytsar frowned, shaking his head. "*Nyet.* I'm staying there until the babe is born, and you need to settle down with a little woman and pop out five kids."

"Five?"

"Absolutely. One for each letter in my given name—in homage to my greatness."

Titov snorted. "Always shouting your own praises."

"If not me, who would?"

Titov chuckled. "That's why you've always succeeded in life. You never doubted yourself. Not like the rest of us."

"How could I when I had such strong support behind me?" Rytsar admitted, trying hard to keep his emotions in check. "I've depended on you all these years. More than you know."

"A trained monkey could have done what I've done," Titov scoffed.

Rytsar punched him again. "You're getting on my nerves with all the self-deprecation."

Titov shrugged. "I guess my sour attitude boils down to one thing."

"What's that?"

"I'm going to miss you."

Titov's honest confession hit Rytsar hard. He grabbed Titov by the back of the neck. Staring straight into his eyes, Rytsar told him, "Your life begins now."

When he let go, Rytsar turned and walked out into the trees. Without looking back, he held up his hand and said, "Five of them." Lowering one finger at a time, he spelled it out for Titov: "A-N-T-O-N."

Laughter followed him as Rytsar escaped into the darkness of the forest to wrestle with his feelings of loss.

Rytsar watched the screen with Captain and Samantha as they flew over Greenland on their way to America.

Using the camera on the military drone, they had a bird's eye view of the compound. Rytsar could barely make out the tiny figures as the Koslov higher-ups made their way into the main building. There they would find the table was laden with rich Russian foods and the finest vodka.

A feast to commemorate their last meal.

It would become immediately apparent to the Koslov brothers that something was off when no one came to greet them. As planned, while a handful of henchmen fanned out with guns raised to search the compound, each brother headed out in a different direction.

Gavriil, ever the militant, headed straight for the ammunition storage. Chuckling to himself, Rytsar watched as Gavriil opened the door and walked inside.

As soon as he set off the laser trigger, he would activate the device and a giant pendulum would swing toward him at great velocity. Gavriil would look down to see Samantha's stiletto heel buried deep in his chest. As he gasped out his last breaths, he would hear the message Rytsar had recorded for the occasion.

Gavriil Koslov, I have waited for this day ever since you ordered my mother's death. Revenge is mine, handed to you in the form of Mistress Clark's stiletto. Welcome to Hell, pizda*, and be sure to say hello to your little brother.*

Rytsar nodded to himself in satisfaction, thinking about it.

Stas, however, took longer to reach his destination.

Since he was in charge of the money, it made perfect sense that he made a beeline to their underground safe, tucked away in the basement of an outlying building.

Rytsar watched with a great sense of anticipation as Stas entered the structure. After making his way down the stairs, Stas would come to the room that held the safe. Once the door was unlocked, Stas would find the room was flooded with a thin layer of water. A lone florescent light above the safe would crackle as it blinked on and off sporadically, highlighting the safe while hiding what lie in wait for him.

Just as with Gavriil, his movement into the room would spell his doom.

As soon as he triggered the laser, he would be hit by a sudden jolt of electricity that would bring him to his knees. The strength of the voltage would keep him still as the device lowered from above, covering his head.

Stas would feel the tight embrace of the helmet as it began to swell, creating a tight seal around his eyes. Meanwhile, the modified fucking machine on wheels would slowly move into position. On the end of it, where there had once been a dildo, there was now a cow's tongue.

Stas would feel the pressure of the suction applied to his eyes steadily increase. However, his screams of terror would be silenced as the cow tongue entered his mouth and the machine began its ramming motion.

As he choked on the tongue, he would hear Rytsar's voice loud and clear inside the helmet.

Stas Koslov, you must pay for my mother's death and for torturing my friend. Revenge is mine today. You will be gifting me your eyes and, because you seem to enjoy tongue so much, I thought you would relish a little tongue action as you breathe your last. Welcome to Hell.

Rytsar felt a sense of immense liberation when the compound disappeared in an enormous explosion a few minutes later, obliterating everything in its wake.

The three of them sat watching the screen in silence afterward.

Slowly the dust began to settle, revealing a massive crater in the middle of nowhere. It was all that was left to signify the end of the Koslov Empire.

It was a sobering and all-encompassing victory.

Heaven

Rytsar stepped off the plane and took in a deep breath.

He had never believed he would feel the warmth of Californian sunshine on his face again. He smiled at his two comrades, feeling a lightness in his heart that he had never known. "It's good to be alive!" he declared.

Both Captain and Samantha nodded their agreement, looking around them in wonder as if they too were in shock to find themselves back home.

"And now I must leave you," Rytsar announced.

Captain clasped his shoulder. "Go in peace."

Rytsar put his hand around Captain's shoulder. "It is because of your expertise that there were no unnecessary deaths. I cannot express the gratitude I feel."

"As I said before, it is rare for a man of my age to be given the opportunity to utilize my talents." He looked at Rytsar thoughtfully. "I have a feeling of closure with my men. Their deaths were not in vain. What I learned after years of war, I was able to employ now. In a sense, our victory was theirs, as well."

"I agree, Captain. Everyone can sleep easier knowing the insanity of the Koslovs has ended. Now go to your woman and let her see you in the flesh. I suspect you will experience a true homecoming tonight."

Captain nodded curtly, but Rytsar saw the glint in his eye. Sex was never so sweet as when it was granted to a dead man.

Rytsar thought of Brie and smiled to himself. Oh, the rapture he was about to experience…

When Rytsar turned to face Samantha, he could see the hint of sadness in her smile. "I'm glad you have returned safely to where you belong, Rytsar."

"Thanks in part to both of you. I will never forget the debt I owe you for my life."

Samantha shook her head. "You owe me nothing but, hopefully, that fresh beginning we spoke about can now become a reality."

Rytsar stared at her for a moment, surprised that he felt no ill will toward her. Given his current state of elation, it was not unexpected, but maybe…just maybe…there was a chance this feeling between them would last.

"Will you be returning to Denver?" he asked her.

"Yes."

Rytsar glanced at his plane. "If you would like, my men can fly you there directly."

Samantha seemed hurt by the suggestion.

"What's wrong?" He felt his hackles rise, suddenly suspicious of her motives toward him and their future.

"I'd like to see Thane and Brie before I go," she answered.

Rytsar laughed at himself, realizing there was no reason to fear. "You may go to them now, if you like. I have someone I must visit before I go to the hospital."

"Before Brie and Thane?" she asked in surprise.

"*Da,*" Rytsar answered, saying no more to her.

Samantha shrugged. "Then I guess I'll head to the hospital. But how should I explain your absence to them? You know they'll be surprised when I show up without you."

He grinned. "Tell them I plan to make a grand entrance."

"Yes," she replied with a half-smile, "they will believe that."

"And if I do not see you again today, know it is good between us."

Her smile transformed into a stunning grin. Echoes of the old Samantha he'd once known flashed in his head as he stared at her.

"I am grateful," she said, then turned away. The controlled Mistress took a moment before turning to meet his gaze. She held out her hand to him. "To new beginnings."

"*Da,* new beginnings," he agreed, shaking her hand.

Rytsar had called in three cars beforehand. He walked to the first and gave his man directions. As the car pulled away, he glanced back at Captain and Samantha. The two were hugging.

Times of adversity made for strange bedfellows.

He found it amusing.

His vehicle pulled up to Marquis's home, but Rytsar felt hesitant to face Wallace again. The burden of his sacrifice was not easy to bear.

However, not one to back down from his responsibility, Rytsar walked up to the door and rang the doorbell. The sound of joyous barking met him on the other side.

Rytsar heard the clicking of tiny nails as the dog rushed to the door, and his eyes suddenly filled with tears of happiness.

"Who is it, girl?" Wallace called out from the other side of the door.

The instant it opened wide enough, *Mudryy* bounded into Rytsar's arms and started licking his face.

Rytsar could do nothing but laugh as the dog covered his face in a hundred canine kisses.

"It is good to see you again," Wallace said, smiling at the excited animal in Rytsar's arms. "Apparently, your pup thinks so too."

Supporting the dog with one arm, Rytsar held out his other to Wallace. The man now wore a leather patch to cover his missing eye. It gave him a distinguished look, much like Captain's.

"I have been anxious to reunite, Wallace."

"You can call me Todd," he replied, ushering him inside, "or Faelan, if you're so inclined."

Rytsar took him up on his offer and asked, "Tell me, Todd, how has your recovery been?"

"You should put *Mudryy* down before she licks your face off." Pointing down the hallway as he closed the door, he said, "We can talk about my recovery once you've a chance to visit with Marquis and Celestia. They're anxious to see you."

When Rytsar set the dog down, she twisted around his legs as he made his way into the living room where Marquis and Celestia stood waiting.

Marquis came up to him first, shaking his hand vigorously. "It is a true miracle to see you again, Durov."

"I feel the same." Rytsar turned his gaze on Celestia and smiled. "I am grateful to see my good friends again."

With a nod from Marquis, Celestia surprised Rytsar by rushing over to him and hugging him tightly. "I've been so worried about you, and have been on my knees, praying for you day and night."

Rytsar looked at her in gratitude. "Your prayers are appreciated, Celestia." He put his hand on his chest, stating, "Truly."

She smiled with tears in her eyes. "I trusted God would hear my prayers, but I am ecstatic they all were answered. *All* of you made it back safely."

"We did," Rytsar answered, but couldn't help glancing at Wallace. 'Safely' was a relative term.

"Please sit down," Marquis instructed, pointing to the couch. On the coffee table, Celestia had already laid out vodka and pickles for him.

He winked at her. "You remembered my favorite kind of coffee."

"I did," she said, blushing as she glanced over at her Master.

"Will you all have a drink with me to celebrate this reunion?" he asked.

"Neither Celestia nor I drink, for personal reasons," Marquis explained. "However, as this is a celebration of a miracle, and Jesus made water into wine, I see no harm in joining you for one drink."

Rytsar looked at the man in admiration. Marquis was an uncompromising soul, and yet he was compassionate and human. Not a pious man of God, but a true living, breathing follower of his faith.

It was inspiring.

Rytsar insisted on pouring the shots and handing them out one by one.

"To you, Celestia, and your untiring prayers," he said, handing her the glass.

Picking up the next, he gave it to Marquis. "For your wisdom of bringing Wallace and I together, and your willingness to take on the responsibility of Lilly in our stead."

He gave the last shot to Wallace.

Rytsar stared straight at him. "To you, Wallace. A man of great courage and uncompromising loyalty. May good fortune shine upon you for the lives you have saved."

Rytsar picked up his own glass and lifted it to them. "To life!"

All four took a drink, but Celestia only lasted one sip. Marquis forced it down in a couple of swallows, while Wallace and Rytsar downed it with similar vigor, slamming their glasses on the table at almost the same moment.

Rytsar roared with exuberance, "Life tastes good, does it not?" He picked up a pickle and bit into it, grinning at the others.

The three each took a pickle and followed suit. Celestia smiled after she ate hers. "I now understand the appeal. I like the sip of vodka with a pickle."

Rytsar let out a hearty laugh and lay back on the couch.

The invitation of a lap proved too much, and *Mudryy* leapt up. Rytsar was about to sweep her off the furniture, but Marquis stopped him, looking at the dog thoughtfully.

"No need to scold her. Her Master is back, and she needs that connection." He looked at Rytsar. "A couch can be cleaned."

Rytsar thanked him, feeling foolish that they were making such a fuss over a dog. But…he was grateful for it. Kissing the top of *Mudryy's* head, he began petting her as she wagged her tail enthusiastically.

"What is the story behind this dog?" Celestia asked. "I know Mr. Wallace told us she helped you, but in what way, may I ask?"

Rytsar looked down at the animal on his lap. *Mudryy* lifted her head and licked him on the chin in response.

A smile crept across his face. "This stray took it upon herself to look after me. I cannot explain why. First, she tried to provide companionship, but I did not want it. Then she became my provider." He patted her head. "She is an excellent thief."

Marquis gave him an amused smile. "We know. She has stolen several items from the table."

Rytsar looked down at the mutt, silently pleased.

"When it seemed that all was lost and there was no chance of escape, this dog…" His voice broke, remembering that moment. "…she chose to stay through the bitter cold so I would not die alone."

He paused for a moment before adding, "You cannot repay someone for that kind of loyalty."

"No, you cannot," Marquis said soberly.

A tear fell onto her head, and *Mudryy* whined.

Rytsar shook his head, petting her again. "For a man who hated animals, I have become…unnaturally attached."

Celestia laughed softly. "It's sweet."

Rytsar turned to Wallace. "Let me ask again. Are you recovering well?"

Wallace nodded. "As you can see, I am now sporting a new fashion accessory. It's all the rage."

"Do not make light of my question," Rytsar cautioned.

Wallace's smiled was relaxed. "I am doing well, Durov."

"You may call me Anton. But I must be blunt with you. After what happened, there is no way I believe you can be doing *well*."

Wallace cocked his head, the eye patch now somehow a natural part of him. "Was it traumatizing? Of course. However, I have been through worse things in my life, Anton. It also helps to know that it was absolutely necessary. No matter how many times I replay it in my mind, I see no other course of action, if we were all to get out of there alive. No one would have survived if a fight had broken out between the two brothers."

"Agreed."

"But it's not just those two things that have helped with my recovery." He looked at the mutt on Rytsar's lap. "*Mudryy* has been a real comfort to me. It's as if she can feel and sympathize with my pain. I can't tell you how much her simple presence is a comfort."

Rytsar knew that truth personally.

Wallace then glanced over at Marquis and Celestia. "Between these two, I have been able to talk through my fears and emotions concerning what happened. After much reflection, I have no doubt I was meant to be there that day. I played out the role I was destined to fulfill."

Wallace turned his attention on Rytsar and smiled warmly. "There is one more thing that has me at peace."

"What's that?"

"Kylie. A girl I met a few months ago, who has turned my life upside down."

"In a good way, I take it," Rytsar said, responding to the expression on Wallace's face.

He leaned forward and answered, "She has been my greatest support, believe it or not."

Rytsar looked at him in surprise, knowing the tremendous influence Marquis Gray had had on him. "Really?"

"Kylie has changed my life in ways I couldn't imagine, but what cemented my admiration of her was her reaction the first time she saw me after…" Wallace pointed to his face.

"Do you mind sharing?" Rytsar asked, now intrigued.

"Not at all," he said, smiling easily. "I had warned

her ahead of time that I'd been injured, but I couldn't bring myself to tell her exactly what had happened—it was too fresh, at the time." He shrugged. "When she came through the door, I expected her to cry or get upset about my eye. But she didn't."

Wallace lay back against the couch. "No, the first thing she did was wrap her arms around me and gaze into my one good eye and tell me, 'You're back in one piece. That's all that matters to me'."

He said nothing for a moment, reining in his emotions. "For reasons I can't fathom, the loss of my eye has meant little to her. She's treated me as if I've always been this way. It makes the adjustment easier."

"That *is* an unusual reaction," Rytsar agreed.

"She is an uncommon woman," Wallace said, smiling once again.

Rytsar reached over the dog to pour another shot, and glanced at Wallace to see if he wanted more. When Wallace nodded, Rytsar filled his up to the brim, as well. They both gulped down the fiery vodka and ate another pickle with gusto.

"So I have no reason to worry about you?" Rytsar pressed.

Wallace smirked. "I'm not saying I don't still have my moments when it flashes in my head and I relive that experience." His brow furrowed, but then he looked to Marquis. "Thankfully, I have people around me to pull me out of it. I'm determined not to live in the past."

"You are a remarkable man, Todd Wallace," Rytsar said with deep sincerity.

Wallace chuckled. "I'm not sure how much of it has

to do with me as a person. I believe circumstances shape us. You either survive them, or they destroy you. In the act of surviving, we develop scars, and those scars help shape us. On rare occasions, such as in my case, those hideous scars help shape you into a better person."

"Wise words," Rytsar complimented him, thinking back on his own life.

"I can't take credit for it." Wallace glanced at Marquis. "He was the one who spoke them to me."

Rytsar nodded to Marquis in respect.

Wallace added with a smirk, "Truth be told, I'd probably be a selfish prick if I hadn't been ripped a few good ones in my life."

Rytsar frowned for a moment, thinking aloud. "I wonder what I would have been like without my past?"

"No need to contemplate," Marquis assured him. "You are who you are now. It cannot be changed, and you are both remarkable people in your own right."

Rytsar let out a low chuckle, reached over *Mudryy* again, and grabbed the bottle of vodka to refill the two glasses, not even asking Wallace if he wanted more.

"Let's drink to our incredible selves," he announced with a grin, raising his glass and clinking it against Wallace's. Rytsar winked at him as he drank it, but his mind was now on other things…

He spontaneously kissed the dog on the nose before standing up. "I am off to see *radost moya* and my brother, Thane."

Celestia clapped her hands together. "How wonderful your reunion will be."

He looked at her for a moment, and the vision of a

small box with blue ribbon came to mind. He suddenly remembered he'd failed to deliver her gift to Thane, and now he had no idea where it was. "I must confess something, Celestia."

Her smile broadened. "Yes?"

"I never gave my comrade the gift, and I have no clue what happened to it."

She batted her eyes sweetly. "I can't believe you even remembered…but you'll be happy to know that Brie found it and gave it to Sir Davis for you. All is well."

"I'm glad to hear it. I'm certain it lifted my comrade's spirit."

"It would be lovely to think it did," she replied, blushing.

"Farewell, good people," he proclaimed as he headed down the hallway, feeling a little drunk—not on vodka—but on the knowledge he was heading to Brie and Thane.

Rytsar took a deep breath before entering the hospital. He felt a little lightheaded, as if he was living in a dream that he would wake up from at any moment.

Braving that first step, he walked into the hospital and headed to the front lobby desk, having forgotten the number of the room. "Can you tell me where Thane Davis's room is? I am his brother."

The receptionist looked up at him, and a slow smile of recognition spread across her face. "Are you Rytsar Durov, the Russian who was kidnapped a few floors up?"

He put his finger to his lips. "No one needs to know who I am."

She grinned, blushing profusely, and whispered, "Of course, Mr. Durov." She wrote the number on a piece of paper and slid it over to him as if she were handing over top-secret files.

"Thank you, *dzyevooshka*."

Her giggle garnered the attention of those around her, so he quickly exited the scene, taking the stairs rather than the elevator.

When he finally reached the door to Thane's room, he could barely contain his excitement. Bursting inside, he yelled, "I'm back from the dead!"

A little old man stared at him in surprise.

"Oh, wait, you're not Thane," Rytsar mumbled.

"No, and if you don't get out of my room, I'm calling security!"

Rytsar raised his hands. "No need for that."

He quickly shut the door and looked at the paper, verifying the number. He stood there, looking confused for several seconds before the movement of a nurse down the hallway caught his attention. Walking over to her, he asked. "Please, where is Thane Davis? I was given this room number."

She looked at the paper. "Oh, the numbers are switched. The room you want is over there." She pointed at the room two doors down.

"Thank you," he said, giving her a curt bow.

Shaking his head in an attempt to regroup before he opened the door, Rytsar walked in. Instead of his triumphant declaration, he remained mute as his gaze landed on Brie, standing beside the bed, and her beautiful round belly.

"Rytsar?" she cried.

Rytsar walked into the room, his eyes locked on Brie. "Oh, *radost moya,* you have grown…" He walked over to her, laying his large hand on her stomach and closing his eyes.

I am back, moye solntse.

Peace washed over him.

He soon felt the gentle hand of Brie cupping his face. "Rytsar…" She choked out his name as she traced his rough jaw with her fingertips.

The urge to kiss her was too strong. He leaned down and planted his lips on hers, the rush of emotion and chemistry cascading over him. When he finally pulled away, he looked at Thane guiltily. "I am sorry. I couldn't resist."

"Hell, I'd kiss you too if that were my thing. Get over here," Thane commanded, slowly pulling himself up in the bed. The two embraced, refusing to let each other go.

It was minutes before Rytsar finally released him. "I'm glad to see you, brother."

"I am too. But, damn it, man, you look terrible. Seriously terrible."

Brie rushed into his arms, burying her face in his chest, her round belly pressed against him. "I can't believe it…" Her quiet sobs filled the room.

Rytsar looked at Thane with a half-grin.

This was heaven.

Unity

"Durov, I'm concerned about you," Thane stated after having a chance to look him over.

Rytsar laughed. "No need, comrade. I am on the mend."

"Well, I want my doctor to look at you, regardless."

He was about to shake his head no, but Brie's look of concern stopped him short. Out of consideration for the babe, he did not want her to waste a second worrying about him.

Sighing, he answered with resignation, "If it will ease your mind."

Brie traced her finger over the long trail of sutures on his right cheek. "What did they do to you?" She ran her hand over his stomach and then wrapped her arms around his waist, commenting, "You're so thin."

When she looked up, he saw tears in her eyes.

"Do not fret, *radost moya*. I survived."

"But at what cost?" Thane asked. "We need to know."

"It might prove too much for *radost moya* to hear

right now. Better to forget."

"But I won't forget," Brie insisted. "I have worried and imagined all kinds of terrible things after speaking with Faelan. I need to know what really happened to ease my mind. I would rather know the truth than for you to keep me in the dark."

Rytsar glanced at Thane, who nodded his agreement.

Sitting down next to the bed, Rytsar pulled Brie onto his lap, needing that physical contact with her.

"After I was taken from here, I was flown by a small aircraft to their secret compound in Siberia. Apparently, I pissed off my captors by insulting the Koslovs, because they were quite free with their physical dislike of me," he explained jokingly.

But his words made Brie whimper. "You insulted them to stop that man from shooting me."

Rytsar glanced at Thane. "See, this is why it is best not to speak of it."

"Brie is simply making connections. Go on," Thane insisted. To Brie, Thane said, "Babygirl, every choice Durov made brought him to this point. He is back with us. Guilt has no place here. In listening to his struggles, you and I only seek to understand what he went through, not to bear a burden of unnecessary guilt."

Brie swallowed back her tears and nodded. With her honey-colored eyes locked on Rytsar, she pleaded, "Please continue."

He looked at her with compassion. "You know if anything had happened to you, my life and the lives of everyone in the room would have ended. I made the only sane choice at the time."

Rytsar then looked at Thane. "Brother, had I known they would storm the hospital, I would never have come that day."

"We know that," Thane answered. "It was never a question."

"By the time I made it to the Koslov compound, I was in bad shape. Very bad." He thought back to that first night and said in an almost wistful voice, "I think I died…"

When he heard Brie gasp, he tilted his head and smiled. "But I heard your voice, *radost moya.* You called out to me and brought me back."

Brie's face became ashen.

"What is it, Brie?" Thane asked.

"I think he is talking about my flogging session with Marquis. I felt Rytsar pulling away from me and screamed out his name."

Brie stared at Rytsar.

"Then it must be so," Rytsar replied easily. At this point, nothing would surprise him. He added with a smirk, "I suppose I must thank Marquis for the timing of your session."

"What happened after you were revived?" Thane asked him.

"The Koslovs kept me in a cell away from the main building and gave me my daily intake of water so that I would die—but not too quickly."

"How long did they keep you like that?" Thane growled under his breath.

"From the day I was brought to them until the day I left. I would have died, had it not been for the stray."

"Yes, Faelan told me about that miraculous little dog. Tell me more," Brie begged.

"Yes, she's a foolish creature who took it upon herself to feed me scraps that she managed to steal."

"Strange that there was a stray way out in the middle of nowhere," Thane commented.

"I have no idea where she came from, but there is no doubt that dog saved my life, comrade. It is the reason I had Wallace bring her back with him."

"That's so beautiful," Brie cooed sweetly.

"So the Koslovs dragged you all the way out to Siberia simply to die?" Thane asked, obviously stunned.

Rytsar sighed loudly, remembering his encounters with Stas.

"I do not believe that was the only reason. I'm certain there were other plans for me, but they were thwarted by my unstable condition."

"Plans?" Thane pressed.

Rytsar glanced at Brie before answering. "I was visited by Stas—alone."

"Ah…" Thane said, a look of concern on his face, knowing what that meant.

"I tried to bite his damn tongue off but, unfortunately for me, I failed to do that and only incited his anger."

"Did he…hurt you, Rytsar?" Brie asked in an agonized voice.

"Hurt my ego? Never. I knew I was irresistible," Rytsar jested, but when he saw her look of devastation, he answered seriously. "His tongue only got as far as my mouth. No one violated me."

Brie rested her head against his arm.

Only Thane knew all the gory details of what happened with Samantha in his dorm room, but Brie had been given the barest of details, so her concern for him now was touching and appreciated.

"My action against Stas almost got me killed a second time. After trying to rip his brother's tongue off, Gavriil decided to abandon me to the elements. I was literally freezing to death when your ransom was accepted and they dragged me out of my cement coffin and into the main building."

Rytsar turned to Thane and smiled. "That was brilliant, by the way. The way you handled my brothers and the Koslovs. But, damn it, peasant," he scolded. "You shouldn't have taken the risk!"

Thane smiled knowingly. "Like you, I made the only sane choice in a volatile situation."

Rytsar had no comeback to dispute the truth of his statement, but he had to know the terms of the ransom. "My brothers have no money, comrade. What did you give to make it the kind of deal the Koslovs would agree to?"

Thane smiled, shaking his head. "Do you remember the island?"

Rytsar felt the blood drain from his face. "You didn't!"

Thane seemed momentarily confused by his reaction, then started to laugh. "No. I did not sell our isle, my friend. What I meant to say was that, like the island, where you kept its worth a secret from me, I mean to do likewise with you. Suffice to say the amount I paid was worth having you here now."

"Let me pay you back," Rytsar pleaded.

"The sacrifice I made was nothing compared to Wallace. I would not dream of it."

Rytsar frowned, but nodded his understanding. "So I take it he explained everything to you?"

Brie's bottom lip trembled. "It was so terrible, what happened…he said you all came close to dying that day."

"*Da*, and we would have, were it not for his bravery. You will be happy to know that Stas repaid his debt before he died."

She shuddered.

Rytsar felt no remorse for the blood on his hands. Every man who had died had deserved to meet his maker that day. If there came a time when he would have to pay for their deaths on Earth or in Hell, he would do it willingly. Without question.

"Wallace told us you were in seriously bad shape when they found you."

Rytsar shrugged. "It could have been worse."

"Yes, you could have been dead," Thane responded somberly. "So how are your injuries healing?"

"I have to be careful, I won't lie. The injuries are slowly healing, except the damn ribs. I'm not happy about the ribs. The physician warned me that my movements might be limited the rest of my life, but that simply cannot be allowed. I *must* heal completely. If I can't reunite with my 'nines…" The thought was too terrible to even finish aloud.

"Let my doctor take a look at you, then," Thane insisted. "She's a forward thinker, and may know of new technology or procedures that may aid with your healing."

"Normally, I would ignore such a suggestion and allow my body to heal on its own, but with my whole way of life in the balance, I must seek help."

"Good, because I don't know how you would survive without your cat o 'nines as your main source of release."

"Me either, brother. I might spontaneously combust from lack of it."

They laughed, but he was actually being serious. The idea that he would never swing his 'nines again terrified him.

Changing the subject, Thane told him, "Captain came earlier with Samantha and explained what happened at the compound."

"It was glorious, *moy droog*!" Rytsar exclaimed with pride. "A work of art."

"That's a strange way to describe an attack," Brie commented.

"Ah, you cannot know the evil that was extinguished that day. There are times when destruction actually promotes life. And this was one of those times."

"Captain shared that you added your own 'flair' to the proceedings."

Rytsar shrugged. "It's true. I felt inspired."

Thane raised an eyebrow.

"I was not going to risk lives, so it necessitated a remote attack. However, it was imperative that the brothers knew why they were dying and who was responsible for it. Revenge is pointless without those two elements."

"Indeed."

"Do you feel safe now?" Brie asked him.

Rytsar smiled at her question. "The Koslovs were an uncontrollable but powerful force in Russia. With their organization destroyed, everything they have built will be divided amongst the different factions of that *bratva*. It will be as if the Koslovs never existed. I do not have to worry about anyone seeking revenge for their deaths. In fact, I am sure there are some who would like to thank me for it."

"Thank goodness no one will be coming for you again," she exclaimed, shuddering.

"So where does that leave you, old friend?" Thane asked.

"As far as my future?"

"Yes."

Rytsar chuckled. "I'm here until that babe graces the world with her presence." He gave Thane a crooked grin, adding, "Of course, only if you'll have me."

"We wouldn't want it any other way."

Brie nodded her head enthusiastically.

"Then the first order of business is for me to get you out of here," Rytsar stated. He loathed doctors and hospitals, and could not handle being there another minute longer than was necessary.

"But Dr. Hessen has already lined up a rehabilitation center. Sir's going to be transferred next week," Brie explained.

"*Nyet.* My brother will not be going anywhere but the apartment," Rytsar insisted.

He directed his next question to Thane. "Wouldn't

you agree that the best place to recover would be in your own home?"

"I would and, I must admit, the idea of returning home so soon has me energized."

"As it should. No man should be cooped up in a white cubicle," Rytsar declared emphatically.

"However, it isn't feasible with the multiple specialists required for my rehabilitation."

"Says who?" Rytsar scoffed. "I will arrange everything. Do not worry."

He turned to Brie, brushing his hand against her soft cheek. "You have suffered for so long, *radost moya*, but now you will be properly cared for by the two men who love you most."

Rytsar was anxious to leave and get everything set up, already mentally ticking off the various things he knew he must arrange for Thane's transfer. The first order of business was to speak with the doctors and nurses and see what else needed to be added to the list.

Rytsar watched Brie's obvious joy as he pushed Sir into the apartment in the wheelchair.

"We're home!" she cried, hugging Sir tightly.

Thane looked up at Rytsar with an expression of gratitude. "Home…at last."

From the back of the apartment came a long yowl, and all three of them watched as the large black cat slowly sauntered out.

"The infamous Shadow," Thane stated.

"One and the same," Rytsar confirmed.

Knowing how the animal had reacted when he first met Rytsar, he was dying to see how the creature would respond to Thane, who was not a man disposed to animals either.

The cat rubbed against Brie's leg first, purring loudly. It then looked up at Thane, twitching its tail and meowing only once.

"I've been told I owe you some thanks, Shadow," Thane told the beast.

Rytsar had to smirk, hearing his comrade talk to the cat as if it were a person.

The cat narrowed his eyes, then rubbed his cheek against Thane's ankle before turning and walking back down the hall.

Rytsar felt rather insulted that the feline hadn't acknowledged his existence, especially after what they had been through together.

Rather than comment on it, however, he said nothing. The last thing he wanted was others to know how he felt being snubbed by a *kot*.

As Thane watched the animal go, he suddenly tensed. "Brie, please tell me you haven't been changing the cat litter."

Brie laughed. "Don't worry, Sir. I always wear gloves and a mask when I do."

"Why?" Rytsar asked, now concerned.

Thane explained, "Cat feces can contain a parasite that causes Toxoplasmosis. Although rare, the infection can cause serious birth defects, or even a miscarriage."

"Oh, hell no!" Rytsar stated. "From now on, only I will change the cat litter."

Brie looked at him guiltily. "Are you sure?"

"I insist."

"Okay," she agreed. "But I want you to know that I talked to my obstetrician and he told me that I would be okay as long as I was careful and washed up thoroughly every time."

Rytsar shook his head. "We take no chances where *moye solntse* is concerned."

"Agreed," Thane replied firmly.

"Fine." She wrapped her arms around Rytsar. "You are now officially my cat litter hero."

"For a cat that doesn't even know I exist," he grumbled.

Brie smiled up at him. "Oh, he noticed you."

Right…

If he must resort to bacon to win back the animal's affections, so be it.

Rytsar rolled Thane to the bedroom and helped him into bed, letting him know that the nurse would arrive in the morning. "Anything you need, anything at all, you just ring this bell," he said, picking it up from the nightstand and giving it a little ring as an example.

"How do you know I won't be an obnoxious patient?" Thane asked him.

"It's true. I am taking my chances, comrade." He grinned. "But every time I feel I'm being taken advantage of, I will spank your sub."

Brie looked at him in surprise. "What?"

"Pray that your Master does not have a hidden sadistic streak, *radost moya*."

She smiled at Thane. "I'd take a million spankings if I had to. I'm just glad to have you back home, Sir."

Thane looked at her with such love that Rytsar felt the need to leave the room. "I will go unpack my things."

Rytsar walked into the spare bedroom and had to stop for a moment. Although the bed was made, it was obvious that nothing had been moved since he'd left it those many weeks ago.

Everything had been carefully preserved as if he'd never left.

Except for the dead flowers…

Those were new.

There they were on the bedside table, a vase of long-dead flowers. He walked over to them and picked up the card attached to read what it said.

Dear Thane and Brie,

I can only imagine how you are feeling right now after what has happened. Please know that my thoughts are with you both, and I am praying with everything within me that he is okay.

If there is anything I can do for you, or if there is any way I can help Rytsar, DO NOT hesitate to call.

Sincerely, Samantha

Rytsar set the card down and looked at the flowers again. He still wasn't sure what to make of Samantha, but one thing was certain; she'd never stopped caring, despite their horrific and complicated past.

While he could never feel any romantic feeling toward her again, he did feel sympathy for the woman. He now better understood why Thane had been steadfast in his friendship with her.

Somehow, his brother had understood Samantha's level of emotional investment in Rytsar. Although Thane had done his best to keep them separated all these years, he'd never severed his relationship with her.

That decision had probably saved Rytsar's life.

He snorted at the irony of it as he unpacked his things and readied himself to go out for the evening.

Home

Rytsar had purposely arranged for a quiet evening for the two, since Thane and Brie needed time to reconnect on a physical level. He'd suspected it had been far too long since they'd been alone together, and it did his heart good to give them this time as a couple.

"Durov," Thane called from his bedroom.

He walked in smiling, ready to receive his friend's gratitude.

"I don't understand. Brie claims you are leaving to go out tonight."

"*Da*."

"Why?"

"Did your concussion make you dense, comrade? I am trying to give you time to fuck your woman in private."

Brie giggled from the floor, already kneeling by the large bed, completely naked, waiting for her scene with Thane to begin.

"I am not the one who is dense."

Rytsar frowned. "What do you mean?" He suddenly

looked at Thane in horror. "You are not…impotent, are you?"

Thane shook his head, looking slightly amused.

"What is it then, *moy droog*?"

"You need something from us."

He laughed. "*Nyet*. I am good, brother."

"No, you are not."

He furrowed his brow, uncertain what Thane was trying to say.

"I need something from you, as well," Brie replied, looking up at him. Her look of love pulled at his heart.

"We would like you to join us tonight."

"I can't," Rytsar protested. "It is your first time alone together."

Brie corrected him. "We have spent many nights together, Rytsar. The nurses have been extremely kind in setting time aside for us to remain undisturbed."

"She's right," Thane assured him. "However, we both thought we'd almost lost you, and you yourself expressed that you didn't believe you were coming back. This physical connection tonight will allow Brie's heart to feel what her mind already knows—that you are home."

That word hit Rytsar in the chest, causing a physical ache.

Home…

"I admit, it sounds too good to pass up."

"Excellent," Thane replied.

Speaking to Brie, Thane commanded, "Undress him, téa."

She smiled at her Master graciously. "I always love it

when you call me by that name, Master."

Brie rocked off her heels with a little more difficulty and stood up. Her round belly was a charming sight to behold.

Rytsar held out his hand to her as she walked over to him. "You are a beautiful little mama."

She smiled up at him as her hands ran over his buttons. She slowly undid the first one, but Rytsar suddenly grabbed her wrist, stopping her. He was hesitant to have them see the number of wounds covering his body, and the many changes to his physique because of the dramatic weight he'd lost.

"What's wrong?" Brie asked gently.

"It is best if I keep my clothes on tonight."

"Nonsense," Thane said from the large bed. "She's going to get to see my sorry ass, so I am sure as hell not going to spare her from yours."

"Rytsar," Brie said, looking up with those big, pleading eyes. "Not to see you would hurt my heart."

He groaned. How she could so easily strip him of his defenses was diabolical.

"Fine, *radost moya*," he sighed in resignation. "But don't say I didn't warn you."

Brie resumed the unbuttoning, slowly pulling back the material of his shirt to expose his bare skin. He saw the concerned look in her eyes even though her smile remained pleasant. He glanced over at Thane, giving him a look of forbearance. This was humiliating for him.

Brie touched every wound and bruise that she found on his skin, and lightly traced the lines of his ribs, which were prominent now. However, her touches did not hurt. They were like a whisper, and he found it somehow healing, as if she were cataloging and accepting each and every one.

When she was done with his upper half, she knelt down and relieved him of his shoes and socks first. She then unzipped his pants.

Rytsar held his breathe as she pulled them down, along with his briefs. Now his wretched body was fully exposed. Just as she had with his torso, she began to run her fingers over him. Rytsar closed his eyes, concentrating on her touch.

"So many wounds," she commented quietly. "Each one reveals a moment you suffered violence." She looked over to Thane, her voice breaking. "There are so many, Master…"

"Téa, he doesn't need your sympathy right now. He needs your love."

She nodded and looked up at him. "I love you, Rytsar."

Her simple words fortified his soul. "I love you too, *radost moya*."

Brie's tactics changed as she smiled up at him seductively and parted those pretty lips. He groaned as she took his hardening cock into her mouth and encased it in warm suction.

Rytsar watched intently as she began to lick and nibble the sides of his cock, causing it to lengthen and ache as she teased it. And she was such a talented cocktease…

When she began to bob her head, her lips moving from the head of his cock to its base, he roared in pleasure. "Yes! Yes!" He fisted her hair to help her along but was soon forced to hold her still, commanding her to stop.

It had been too long.

He looked at Thane. "I'm as horny as a rutting boy."

Thane chuckled. "Feel free to give in to your boyish desires."

"*Nyet*." He held out his hand and helped Brie to her feet. "We should join you on the bed and see if we can't get this submissive to come."

He led Brie over to Thane. "But first you must get your Master in the same state I am."

Brie smiled at Thane as she slowly removed each piece of clothing, doing it in such a manner that it was seductive and alluring. Rytsar was not surprised to see Thane's atrophied muscles, a product of being still for so long.

But there was one thing both of them had in common—hard shafts. No matter the shape of their individual bodies, their cocks were rigid and proud.

A direct result of the beautiful girl in the room.

"*Radost moya*, it's only fair that you suck your Master's cock," Rytsar stated, wanting Brie to ramp up Thane's state of arousal to the same level.

He didn't want to be the only one struggling for control over his libido.

Without hesitation, Brie climbed onto the bed. Her round belly made it impossible for her to kneel between his legs, so she lay on her side, propping herself up to take his shaft into her mouth.

Rytsar smirked when he saw the look on Thane's face. That girl had definitely learned her way around a man's cock with that talented mouth. A far cry from the first time he'd experienced her oral skills.

He watched with satisfaction as his comrade tried to keep his need to orgasm in check. It wasn't long before he was commanding her to stop, as well.

Thane was a man of great control, so his lack of restraint now only highlighted how badly this session was needed—by all of them.

Rytsar lay down next to Brie on the bed so that she was sandwiched between them.

She settled down on her back, looking at both of them excitedly.

"And now we get down to the business of making téa scream in ecstasy," Thane stated.

"*Da*," Rytsar growled, going for her breasts.

When Thane's hand disappeared between Brie's legs, Rytsar felt her stiffen, as he began flicking her clit with expert hands that knew her so well.

Rytsar sucked on one nipple while playing with the other. His cock ached with the simple stimulation as she responded eagerly to his attention.

A dead man risen, his body *needed* to plant its seed deep inside her.

Apparently, she was as turned on as they were, because her first orgasm rushed through her as she cried out in passion.

His balls tightened at the sound of her pleasure, and he had to rein in his own climax. Rytsar growled in frustration, biting her on the neck hard enough to bruise the skin. She reacted by pressing his head down on her nipple.

He grunted in animal-like fervor as he sucked harder.

Thane must have been vigorously rubbing her G-spot, because the next orgasm was on her and more intense than the first. She whimpered afterward, her pussy gushing with sweet, watery come.

"Oh, my God…oh, my God…" she moaned.

Both he and Thane had resorted to stroking their cocks in response to her enthusiastic climax.

Rytsar stared at her breasts. "Your breasts…they have grown since I've played with them last." He grasped one in his hand, admiring the extra fullness of it. "I look forward to the babe being born so I can taste your mother's milk."

Brie turned to him, her eyes wide. "Really?"

"Oh, yes," he growled. "I have fantasized about it on many occasions."

Brie turned to Thane. "Have you?"

He smirked. "The thought has crossed my mind."

Brie grasped her boobs, pressing them together as she looked down at them lustfully. "To have two men suckling my breasts at the same time? I could come just thinking about it. How weird is that?"

Rytsar chuckled hoarsely. He had to remind himself not to come after seeing her willingness. "Not weird at all, *radost moya.*"

He kissed her nipple, promising himself s*omeday soon…*

"May I pleasure you both at once?" she asked innocently.

Rytsar looked over at Thane, and they both nodded their agreement.

She quickly changed position, turning to face them as she knelt between them. Taking one in each hand, Brie began to stroke their hard cocks.

Rytsar closed his eyes, giving in to the tight hold she had as her hand moved up and down his shaft with a twisting motion. Even her hand jobs were exceptional after years of guided practice.

The ache in his loins soon became too much, and he cried out huskily, "I'm coming." His come burst from his manhood in impressive bursts that shot into the air, landing on his stomach and chest.

It appeared Thane was not to be outdone. When Rytsar opened his eyes he saw that his comrade too was covered in come, and Brie…she was grinning in triumph.

She quickly slipped off the end of the bed and got wet towels, thoroughly cleaning both men off.

Once she was settled between them again, the two went back to work on her. This time they coordinated their efforts, first playing with her breasts as they took turns kissing her. However, this time they moved much more slowly, wanting to build up her climax in order to challenge her with it.

"Téa, you are not allowed to come until Durov gives the word," Thane told her.

She frowned, looking at Rytsar with concern. "But you are a sadist."

He laughed wickedly. "I am…"

Rytsar felt her muscles tense. She knew what she was in for. With both men sated and her own level of need heightened, it would be easy to torture her with his love.

Rytsar began to nibble, pinch, and pull on her left

nipple, making her squirm from the more intense stimulation. He found her unusually receptive to his touch. He then covered her throat in love bites before sinking his teeth into the most sensitive area.

Brie moaned loudly as Thane rolled her right nipple between his fingers, tugging lightly as Rytsar held her in that possessive pose like a predatory cat playing with its food before the final bite.

They continued their attentions as they moved slowly toward her pussy, leaving a trail of kisses and bites on her thighs, which were spread wide for them.

Of like minds, both men returned to her breasts as their hands made short work of her swollen pussy. Thane's fingers entered her cunt as Rytsar teased the rim of her ass.

Conscious of the babe in her belly, they were going to give her a different version of DP.

Brie was breathing in short, shallow gasps, her impressive chest rising and falling rapidly as Rytsar slowly eased his finger inside her tight hole. She was noticeably hotter than before, the result of her pregnancy.

Rytsar could only imagine what it would feel like to sink his dick deep into those flames of desire.

He groaned out loud at the thought, his cock already preparing itself for such an onslaught.

The sound of his pleasure caused her pussy to start pulsating in response.

"Do not come, *radost moya.* Don't disappoint me."

She held her breath, her whole body tensing as she tried to stave off the orgasm about to overtake her.

Thane took pity on his submissive and pulled his

hand away, placing his wet fingers on her lips instead and commanding, "Lick."

Refocusing her attention helped her regain control. She licked and sucked her Master's fingers seductively, her climax abating for the time being.

Rytsar didn't mind Thane's distraction. The truth was, he was hungry to feel her come again, but it was important to him that the two connect.

"*Radost moya*, make love to your Master while I watch."

Rytsar lay back in a comfortable position as he watched Brie carefully straddle Thane. The belly made things a little more challenging for her but, damn, it looked cute on her.

Brie looked down at her Master adoringly. She mouthed the words *I love you* as she rubbed her wet pussy over his hardening shaft. It didn't take long until he was erect again and he commanded she take him.

Brie lifted herself up to position his cock against her opening. Closing her eyes, she moaned as she slowly lowered herself onto his cock.

Bracing herself against his chest, she began rocking against him.

"You feel so good, téa," he commented.

"After all those months apart, I don't think I can ever get enough of your cock, Master."

He grunted as she shifted her position and took him a little deeper. She ground her pussy in a circular motion, making him groan in pleasure.

Watching the way she was servicing his comrade's cock made Rytsar hungry for Brie. Moving closer, Rytsar ran his hand over her back, settling on her firm buttocks. He slapped her ass, causing her to cry out in delight.

"You like that, do you?" he growled huskily, rubbing the other ass cheek before slapping it.

Thane grabbed her wrists and pulled her down toward him, exposing that sensual area between the valley of her ass cheeks.

Rytsar took that as an invitation and started stroking the sensitive skin of her tantalizing rosette with his finger.

"Oh, Rytsar," she moaned in encouragement.

As she continued to fuck Thane, Rytsar circled the rim of her ass before slipping his finger inside while he kissed her on the lips. He was again surprised by how hot her internal temperature was, and it excited him to think of his own cock claiming that fiery body soon.

Brie moaned with passion as he fingered her ass while biting down on her shoulder. His need for her grew as the rhythm of her rocking increased. Thane grabbed onto her hips to guide her movements, throwing his head back as he let out a low groan.

His enjoyment encouraged Brie to rock even faster. Suddenly, her whole body tensed and she stopped.

"You may come, *radost moya*…" Rytsar growled.

Brie moved her lips toward him, kissing him deeply as her body shuddered in an orgasm.

Rytsar felt the warm gush of her excitement on his hand and growled into her mouth.

When Thane started her movements back up, Brie broke away from Rytsar and looked down at her man. "You are so sexy, Master."

"I love it when you come all over my cock," he responded lustfully. "So much so, I feel the need to release my love inside you."

Her eyes flashed with excitement and desire. "Yes, please!"

With his eyes locked on Brie's, Thane slowed down her movements, slowly building up his own orgasm.

Rytsar pulled away from Brie, allowing the couple this private moment as Thane found release inside his woman. It was a beautiful sight, and Rytsar lay back on the bed, pleased to have been a part of it.

Afterward, Brie kissed her Master on the nose before disengaging and rolling off the bed to disappear into the bathroom.

"I can't wait until I'm strong enough to fuck her. While I love her on top, I long to take her from behind and slam my cock into her pussy."

Rytsar smirked. "That is good motivation to work hard."

"Indeed."

Thane looked down at Rytsar's rock-hard manhood and commented, "It looks as if you're in need of my sub's attention again."

"I am."

"How would you like her?"

Rytsar chuckled wickedly, the sadist in him begging to play. "Do you mind if I challenge *radost moya*?"

"As long as you keep the baby's health in mind, I have no issues."

Rytsar looked at him in shock. "I would *never* do anything to harm the babe."

Thane smiled. "No need to get offended, old friend. I would rather err on the side of caution when it comes to Brie and the baby."

"Naturally." Rytsar felt slightly appeased. "But you and I are one when it comes to the babe. Nothing and no one will hurt her," he said vehemently.

Brie came out of the bathroom freshened up and ready to continue. She knelt before them, head bowed, awaiting her next command.

Rytsar said with an evil smirk, "*Moy droog,* do you have clovers?"

Brie's head popped up, her eyes wide with fear.

"I do."

"*Radost moya*, would you get them for me?" Rytsar commanded.

Brie whimpered, but stood up and opened the closet door to search for the dreaded clamps. Her frighten voice came from the closet. "Sir, you and I have never used them before. Where would they be?"

"In the third drawer. Back compartment," Thane answered smoothly.

Brie came out of the closet with the silver clamps in hand, but before she climbed onto the bed to rejoin them, she stopped and dropped her gaze to the floor.

"Respectfully, Rytsar, I think you should know that my breasts have become more sensitive since becoming pregnant."

"Good."

She looked up in surprise.

"What? Did you think that would sway me?" He held out his hand to take the clips, explaining, "They will not damage your sensitive nipples, simply stimulate them."

"To the point of tears," she cried.

"Precisely."

Brie glanced at Thane.

He answered her silent plea with, "You can always use your safeword, babygirl. Even before play begins."

Brie looked back at Rytsar with a worried expression.

"We have played with these before," he said seductively, shaking the metal clamps. "It will be fun."

She stuck out her bottom lip. "For you."

He chuckled warmly, reminding her, "Did you not come gloriously last time we used them?"

She sighed and nodded.

"So trust your Russian lover, and come to bed." He patted the area between him and Thane.

Brie looked from one man to the other, hesitating for only a few moments before climbing back onto the bed.

"Now that there are two of us, we can place them on both nipples at the same time. You should enjoy that."

She whimpered again.

Rytsar grabbed her chin and turned her head toward him.

She stared into his eyes fearfully.

"This isn't about me forcing you, *radost moya*. This is about you embracing the sensation I wish to give with an underlying sense of courage and trust."

She nodded, but shuddered when he placed the cold metal clamps on her bulging stomach.

"We will not begin until you give the word."

Both men went back to kissing, nuzzling her neck,

and teasing her nipples while Rytsar gave her time to work through her inner resistance.

His cock was already throbbing, the power exchange with her as sweet and erotic as he remembered from the last time.

Rytsar felt her slow down her breathing as she swallowed down her fears for him. It was a gradual surrender, but there finally came a point where she was ready. He could sense it, and groaned in pleasure.

Brie picked up a nipple clamp in each hand and gave one to each man.

She closed her eyes and announced, "Please," in a confident voice.

"Look at me, téa. I want to see those pretty eyes," Thane told her.

She opened them and smiled nervously at him. "Yes, Master."

Rytsar was pleased to see how hard her nipples were. Fear had that effect on a woman's body, which made it easier to attach the wicked clamps.

He and Thane coordinated the timing, opening the clovers wide and placing both ends against either side of a nipple. Then Rytsar counted down for added fun and anticipation. "*Tri, dva, odin…*"

They released their hold on the metal clamps simultaneously and watched the ends close cruelly on her pink nipples as Brie arched her back and screamed.

"Oh, my God…oh, my God…oh, my God!"

"She said that when she came earlier, but it had a different ring to it," Rytsar joked with Thane.

Thane smiled at him.

His comrade responded to Brie's pain by gazing into her eyes, stroking her hair, and hushing her gently as she grew used to the painful pressure of the clamps.

"I like this dynamic between us, comrade. It's like you are the good cop and I am the bad cop," Rytsar stated.

Grinning devilishly at Brie, he added, "And I do so enjoy playing the bad cop for you, *radost moya*." He tweaked the chain a little, inciting another round of "Oh, my Gods."

As much as he enjoyed teasing her with the clamps, he could not deny he was desperate to claim her. He *needed* to fill her up with his cock and show her just how deep his love really went.

Springing off the bed, Rytsar pulled her around so her legs were dangling off the edge and her head was next to Thane's.

"Kiss her while I penetrate this fiery pussy," he growled lustfully.

Brie tilted her had back and Thane began kissing her deeply with his tongue.

Rytsar spread her legs wide and stared down at her gorgeously wet and swollen cunt. "I have missed your body."

Brie looked up for a moment, tears still in her eyes from the pressure of the clamps, and told him in earnest, "I have missed you terribly."

The truth behind her words was not lost on him. Although this was a scene, there were intense emotions attached to their reunion.

He put them aside, rubbing his cock up and down

her slick pussy, readying her for penetration by coating his shaft with her wet juices.

When he could hold back no more, he slid his shaft into her heaven slowly. In a paradox of sensations, chills went up his spine as her fiery heat engulfed his cock.

He roared like a conquering lion.

Rytsar stroked her pussy, slowly and purposely, building up the intensity for both of them. Her G-spot was swollen, and her pussy so incredibly hot. Brie pushed her hips into him, inviting him to take her even deeper.

Quite conscious of her delicate condition, Rytsar savored the tightness it caused, but allowed Brie to gauge the level of depth. Thankfully, she not only wanted, but could still take, his full shaft, given a little time and persistence.

Rather than giving in to the urge to pound her, Rytsar stroked her with his length, concentrating on her G-spot as he built her orgasm with each thrust.

He noticed Thane playing with the clamps, making her squirm and wiggle underneath Rytsar. It only turned him on more, and he found himself on the edge again.

Grabbing her hips with both hands, Rytsar looked down at Brie, watching the way the heavy chain danced across her chest. Adjusting the angle of his shaft, Rytsar was able to give her exactly what she needed for a massive orgasm. With all her senses focused on his cock rubbing her G-shot, and her Master's tongue in her mouth, Brie was no longer concentrating on the clovers he was eyeing so hungrily.

He gritted his teeth, wanting to time it perfectly for

her. After three solid strokes, he suddenly stopped and let her pussy take over as it pulsated harder and harder until she reached her peak and the first contraction from her orgasm milked his cock. At that precise moment, he grabbed the chain and yanked it, watching her nipples as they were pulled with it, while thrusting his cock into her.

Her passionate screams filled the room as he came long and hard inside her, load after load of his seed bathing her insides. He collapsed on top of her, giving one last thrust, and then became completely still.

Rytsar continued to feel her rhythmic contractions as she came, her orgasm lasting much longer. When she opened her eyes again, they were glazed over with the look of a woman in subspace.

"She's flying high," Thane commented, gently stroking her face.

"*Radost moya* took the clovers well this time."

Thane chuckled. "I don't think she will ever request them without prodding, but she does seem to enjoy the results."

"I agree, *moy droog*," Rytsar said proudly, leaning down to kiss her.

He helped reposition her next to Thane, his ribs protesting as he did so. "Take care of her for me," he said.

Rytsar took a quick shower, letting the warm water run over his beaten and battered body.

By the time he returned to their bed and lay beside Brie, he could see that she was slowly coming down from her high.

Brie turned her head and stared at him, an intoxicated smile on her lips. "That was…"

"A good, hard come for you," he answered.

She shook her head slowly.

He looked at Thane with amusement. "Do you think she meant yes?"

Thane chuckled. "Who knows?"

Rytsar sighed deeply. "This was a good thing."

"It was needed," Thane replied. "For all of us."

Rytsar nodded, suddenly overcome with strong emotions. He turned his head away, trying to regain control, but it was as if he was crashing much like a sub after an intense high, and he had no way to stop it.

"What's wrong?" Thane asked.

Rytsar shook his head.

The reality of what he had been through and how close he'd come to losing Thane, Brie, and the babe hit him like a physical blow to the chest. He couldn't catch his breath from it.

When he felt Thane's hand on his shoulder, it seemed to break Rytsar's resistance and he started to cry, his tears falling without restraint.

As a tidal wave of pain and grief washed over him, Rytsar began to sob quietly, unable to stop it.

Brie immediately spooned against him, her belly pressed against his back.

Her sobs soon joined his own.

Thane responded by wrapping his arm around them both, holding them in a reassuring embrace.

"You are home, brother."

Making Amends

Rytsar went back to his room to rest, and was startled to find Shadow sitting on the top of the dresser in the corner of the room.

The cat made no sound or movement, but its eyes followed him wherever he went in the room.

It was uncanny, and a little creepy.

Apparently, Brie had been correct. The cat did know Rytsar was there, but he could not begin to guess what was going on behind the big yellow eyes of that devil cat.

"You are a strange one, Shadow," Rytsar confessed. "The way you're looking at me so intently leaves me to wonder if your plan is to stare me down until I cry uncle. Sorry, old tom, I've won every staring contest I've ever been a part of. You'd better come up with a different plan or prepare to lose."

Rytsar stared hard at the beast, thinking it would look away as animals were prone to do.

It did not. In fact, the feline didn't move or respond at all.

Finally, Rytsar gave up trying to interact with it and

went to bed, already determined to cook up some bacon in the morning.

One way or another, he would get that cat to respond to him.

In the morning he woke up suddenly, sweating and barely able to breathe. He felt a wave of panic as his mind raced to determine where he was and what was happening.

It took a few seconds to realize the cat had curled up next to his face with its front paws lying across his neck.

As soon as he moved his head, the cat started purring.

Rytsar moved his head away from the animal, staring at it questioningly. "Were you trying to kill me just now?"

The cat narrowed its eyes and continued purring.

Although he didn't sense any animosity from the animal, Rytsar had no idea why it would be sitting on his face trying to smother him.

He left the bed, with the animal following him with its eyes as he got dressed.

"*Radost moya?*" he called out to Brie when he exited the room.

"Yes, Rytsar?" she asked, smiling at him as she rubbed cocoa butter on her stomach.

"Your cat tried to assassinate me."

She stopped what she was doing and looked at him, laughing, obviously not believing him. "I wondered what had happened to him last night."

"It sat on my face, trying to extinguish my last breath, while it laid its paws on my throat."

Shadow came out of the bedroom as if he knew he was the subject of the conversation.

"I'm sure he was just letting you know he's glad to see you."

He looked at her incredulously. "He tried to kill me."

Brie shook her head and went to the kitchen, opening up the fridge. She took out a small can and a spoon from the utensil drawer. "Do you remember that you sent Shadow a lifetime supply of caviar? We get a shipment every week."

"I do recall making that request of Titov."

"Well, whenever I feed it to him, I always have something of yours for him to smell. Kind of like what you did with me and Sir's shirt when we scened together at the cabin."

Rytsar smirked. "What are you saying, *radost moya*?"

"The reason Shadow wasn't surprised when you showed up here was due to the fact he smells you every day when I give him a spoonful of caviar. I'm sure last night he was just saying thank you."

She handed Rytsar the can and spoon and smiled at him.

"You did this every day?"

"Of course. I wanted him to know who the gift was from."

Rytsar shook his head and leaned down to kiss Brie on the nose before he turned his attention to the cat.

"So you appreciated my thank you gift, after all?" He sat down cross-legged, spooned a small portion of caviar for the cat, and held it out to him. "I will always be indebted to your claws and bravery, Shadow."

The cat moved closer to him and took a dainty lick of the black eggs.

"I am a man who repays his debts."

The cat looked at him for a moment before licking the rest of the spoonful and purring.

"He always purrs when he eats that stuff," Brie informed him.

"Of course," Rytsar said, taking a spoonful himself. "Caviar is a decadent treat."

Brie stared at him with her mouth open.

"What?" he asked, surprised by the expression on her face.

"You just ate from the spoon after feeding Shadow."

He shrugged. "That's what starving to death will do to a person."

Brie knelt down beside him and gave him a hug. "I hope you never have to feel hungry again."

Rytsar grinned. "I won't if these shipments keep up." He fed another spoonful to Shadow but said in all honesty, "Thank you for keeping my memory alive with this beast."

Her bottom lip trembled. "I wasn't sure you would ever come back, but I never gave up hope."

He kissed the top of her head, wrapping his arms around her. "Thank you, *radost moya*."

Brie pressed against him, her round belly making its presence known. That's when he felt the first kick. He looked down at her stomach in wonder, placing his hand on it.

Sure enough, he felt the movement again and grinned. Leaning closer to Brie's stomach, he said, "I feel you, *moye solntse*. Your *dyadya* is here."

Brie's eyes sparkled. "Yes, her *dyadya* is here."

He looked at her moving stomach and shook his head in awe. "It truly is a miracle, *radost moya*."

Brie rubbed the area where the babe was kicking. "I agree, but I wish the little miracle would take pity on her mama and stop kicking so hard."

Rytsar looked proudly at her belly. "She kicks because she is strong."

Brie pressed against the tiny bulge. "Well, this strong girl is leaving a bunch of bruises inside my tummy. At least, that's what it feels like," she laughed.

"But you will bear it because you are her mother and you want her to be strong."

"I *want* her to take pity on me," Brie insisted. "Not that I have any say in the matter."

Rytsar gazed down at her stomach again, not hiding his pride. "We should go show Thane how active she is right now."

Thane must have been listening to their conversation, because he was leaning against the headboard waiting for them, when they walked into the room.

"Sorry if we woke you, Sir," Brie said, leaning over to give him a peck on the lips.

"I hear that you've been admiring our energetic child," Thane told Rytsar with a grin.

"I have been, *moy droog*. I'm heartened to know she is so robust."

"She's a Davis and a Bennett. Nothing can stop her," Thane said with satisfaction.

Rytsar frowned for a moment, uncertain what their

answer would be, but determined to ask. "When it is time…will I be allowed to see her birth?"

Brie looked at Thane questioningly.

He smiled. "That is up to the little mother. Her word is law when it comes to the birth."

Brie giggled. "I guess Sir is giving me full reign to top from the bottom in this matter."

Rytsar smiled charmingly at her, and asked again, "So, *radost moya*, what is your answer?"

She shook her head, rolling her eyes as she did so. "Of course we want you there. I would be hurt if you weren't with us."

Rytsar grasped her stomach in both his hand and leaned down again. "Did you hear that, *moye solntse?* Your *dyadya* will be there when you greet the world."

Thane chuckled. "Just so we're clear, old friend. I'm the one cutting the umbilical cord."

Rytsar put a hand on Thane's shoulder. "Brother, I am only there to witness the wondrous event. You are her father, and *you*," he said, kissing Brie on the forehead, "are her beautiful mother."

Rytsar stood up and faced them both. In a solemn vow, he put his hand on his chest. "I will be the best *dyadya* a man can be. Not only in *moye solntse's* eyes, but in the eyes of both of you. If you ever find fault with my actions, you have only to tell me and I will correct it."

Brie looked at Rytsar lovingly while Thane spoke for them both. "We gladly accept your commitment to our daughter. Would you like to know her name now?"

Rytsar shook his head. "*Nyet.* I want you to formally introduce her to me when you place the babe in my arms."

"Aww..." Brie cooed sweetly. "You really are going to make the very best *dyadya*."

"I take my role seriously, *radost moy*—"

Rytsar was interrupted by rapid knocking at the front door.

"That must be your nurse," he informed Thane. Looking at Brie's naked body, and then at Thane's, he said with a grin, "So I guess I ought to be the one to answer that."

"Please give me time to get us dressed and the place picked up a bit," Brie told him, rushing to pick up their scattered clothing from off the floor.

"Just throw me a pair of boxers, Brie," Thane told her. "I'll struggle into them while you throw on a dress and tidy up."

"I can help you into them," Rytsar offered, glancing at the door as the person knocked a second time.

"No. I need to reclaim my independence, and it begins today with this damn underwear," Thane stated emphatically.

Brie quickly handed him a pair before rushing into the closet to dress.

Rytsar glanced around the bedroom proudly. It was in a shambles and definitely looked like they'd had a good time the night before.

"I wouldn't worry about the room, *moy droog*. Better the nurse know now what kind of man you really are."

Rytsar chuckled as he turned, laughing, and walked down the hallway to answer the door.

He couldn't stop smiling at the idea of being granted

the ultimate privilege of being there when *moye solntse* was born.

There was nothing more he could want of the world.

When he opened the front door, his hackles rose in alarm at the sight of two large and muscular men. One happened to be carrying a large duffle bag at his side.

"Can I help you?" he asked defensively.

"We're here for Mr. Davis."

Rytsar didn't budge as he stared them down.

"Hello, I'm his day nurse," one of them said, holding out his hand.

"And I'm the physical therapist," the other finished, also holding out his hand. "I personally believe in arriving early, because morning exercises help my patients throughout the day."

Rytsar looked them up and down before shaking their hands. He grinned as he stepped back and invited them inside.

"I didn't realize you would both come at the same time, but welcome," he stated, now very curious about what Thane's reaction would be to these two men.

Brie came out of the bedroom in a pretty little dress and stopped short when she saw the two muscular bodies in front of her.

"Is everything okay?" she asked in a concerned tone.

"Yes, *radost moya*. These men are Thane's nurse and physical therapist."

A smile suddenly spread across her face as she came forward. "We greatly appreciate you coming to our home."

"Of course, Mrs. Davis."

"And your name is?" Brie asked the man with the curly brown hair.

"James Hill. I will be your husband's nurse for the duration. You can call me James."

Brie shook his hand vigorously and then turned to the man with sandy blond hair.

"I'm Kyle Evans, physical therapist. I prefer to be called by my surname."

"Certainly, Mr. Evans," Brie replied, taking his hand.

She smiled at Rytsar before turning back around and leading them down the hall to the bedroom. "If you'll follow me, I'll show you to your new patient, Sir Thane Davis."

It was obvious Brie was pleased with the medical staff, but Rytsar followed behind, wanting to catch a glimpse of Thane's initial reaction.

"Sir, this is James and Mr. Evans. They're here to provide you with the medical assistance you need."

Thane looked at them and nodded, no other reaction on his face. "Excellent."

He pulled back the sheet, exposing that he was in nothing but his boxers. "I could use some help to the bathroom, if you don't mind."

Rytsar noticed Brie stepping back and watching with enthusiasm as the muscular James helped Thane out of bed and to the restroom.

He noticed she was biting her lip and suspected he knew where her mind was headed as she watched.

The physical therapist started setting his equipment out on top of the chest of drawers. It reminded Rytsar of a Dom setting up a scene, and he smiled to himself.

Thane was going to be in for a good time.

"I think it best if we leave the professionals to their work while we get Thane something for breakfast," Rytsar suggested.

"But Sir doesn't eat breakfast," Brie reminded him.

Mr. Evans looked up and told her, "He will now. His body cannot rebuild the muscles he needs without a proper diet."

"Well, omelets are out of the question." Brie burst out laughing.

Rytsar joined her, putting his arm on her shoulder. "I'm sure you can come up with something nutritious he will eat."

As they walked to the kitchen, she whispered to Rytsar, "Did you purposely choose those two men?"

Rytsar shook his head. "I used the agency your doctor recommended. I had no idea who would be showing up this morning."

"Well, I certainly have no complaints."

Rytsar smirked. "No doubt. I could see it on your face."

"I'm not ashamed to admit that seeing my handsome Sir with two big, burly men is exciting."

"I wonder how your Master feels."

"He didn't seem to have much of a reaction."

"I noticed that, as well."

Brie quickly threw together a simple breakfast of sliced apple, toast, and blueberry yogurt. She arranged it prettily on a plate and looked up for Rytsar's approval.

"I wouldn't eat it."

She giggled as she headed down the hall. When she

came back a few minutes later, she had a shocked look on her face.

"What did he say?" Rytsar asked.

"He personally picked those men, Rytsar. That's why he didn't react when he saw them. Sir told me he wanted the strongest help available because he plans to recover as quickly as possible."

"The man is a control freak," Rytsar complained good-naturedly.

"Lucky me, I get to admire the eye candy the whole time he recovers."

"Four men and one girl. I could see how that would be a woman's dream."

Brie blushed. "I wasn't thinking like that."

"Well, I was," he replied, already imagining the dynamics of her taking four at once.

Brie rolled her eyes. "The two of you are more than enough for me."

"Still, it's fun to imagine, isn't it?"

"I have more important things to think about."

"Like what?" he challenged teasingly.

"I should be getting back to work on my second documentary, but I was thinking of going back to my pet project instead."

"And what pet project is that?"

"I want to make a film about Sir's father, Alonzo."

"I approve," he said with a nod. "It is a fine idea. I know your Master will appreciate it."

She grinned. "I think so too."

Rytsar was surprised to hear yet another knock at the door.

"Are you expecting anyone?" Rytsar asked her.

Brie frowned. "No, especially this early in the morning."

Rytsar approached the door cautiously, his instincts telling him there was trouble on the other side. He took a quick peek through the peephole and saw an older couple standing there. It took him a few seconds to recognize Brie's parents.

Neither wore pleasant expressions.

"Hold on, Mrs. Davis," he warned Brie. "Things are about to get bumpy for you."

Brie looked worried. "What do you mean?"

Rytsar swung the door open and smiled broadly at them both. "Welcome, Mr. and Mrs. Bennett. How nice to see you again."

Brie's father glared at Rytsar for a moment, the circumstances of their last encounter during the wedding still clearly scorched in his mind.

"What a shock to find you here, Mr. Durov," Brie's mother said. "The last I heard, your whereabouts were still unknown. By the looks of it, you've had an extremely rough time of it."

"I'm fortunate to have an army of loyal friends and the constitution of a horse, Mrs. Bennett. Thank you for your concern." He invited them both inside, interested in seeing how this would play out.

Brie ran up to her parents, hugging her mother first and chiding, "Why didn't you tell me you were coming?"

"Why would we?" her father huffed angrily. "You would have just put us off again. We're tired of being brushed off by our daughter. We're your parents, for

Christ's sake."

Brie hesitated, put off by the force of his anger but hugging him just the same.

Her mother grabbed Brie back and held her tight, tears flowing down her cheeks. "It's been too long. Way too long, Brie."

Rytsar could see Brie relaxing in her mother's arms, and he felt a tinge of jealousy. What he wouldn't give to feel the arms of his mother again. But jealousy had no place here. "I will leave you," he stated, trying to make a quick exit.

"No, Rytsar, please stay with me," Brie begged.

Even though her father shot daggers when he turned around, Rytsar moved back to her side, determined to be there for her.

When Marcy pulled away, she looked down at Brie's belly and shook her head in amazement. "Look how big you've gotten! What are you, six months now?" Her tears started up again as she looked at her husband. "I can't believe how much I've missed."

Her father growled at Brie, "You have been very unkind to your mother, young lady."

"Mom, Dad…please sit on the couch. It's time we had a heart-to-heart talk."

"It's far past time," her father snapped.

Rytsar had a hard time keeping his opinions to himself. Although he understood the source of the man's anger, anything that might upset *radost moya* was unwelcomed in this home.

"Daddy, please. I need your understanding, not your anger."

He snarled as he sat down. "What? Are we supposed to simply accept that you cut us out of your life as soon as Thane had that accident? When you needed us the most, you became cold and distant. Maybe I can handle such shoddy treatment by my own child, but it's not fair to your mother. She didn't deserve any of this, and you should be ashamed of yourself."

"Please, Bill. Let's not get off on the wrong foot," Marcy pleaded.

Instead of backing down, her father stared at Rytsar and demanded harshly, "Brianna, where is your husband right now?"

"He's in the bedroom doing physical therapy, Daddy. Rytsar arranged it so Thane could come home and recover here."

Marcy took it as an opportunity to hold out an olive branch to her by saying, "That's wonderful, honey. I can only imagine how sick he must be of that hospital. I'd be happy to help you in any way I can by cooking, cleaning, running errands…whatever you need."

Rytsar was growing to like this woman.

"Mom, I'm finally getting my life back to normal. As much as I appreciate—"

"Brie, is that your parents that I hear?" Thane called from the bedroom.

"It is, Sir."

"Please ask them to come join me."

Brie looked at her parents and smiled. "Sir would like to see you both."

"At least someone expresses a desire to see us," her father mumbled under his breath.

"Wonderful," Marcy replied, grabbing her husband's hand. "We've been very anxious to see Thane."

They walked into the room to find Thane fully dressed, the two men holding him up as he struggled to take a step. He was looking down at his feet, but glanced up at Brie's parents and smiled. "It's going to be a long road ahead, but I am determined to fully recover as soon as possible."

Brie's mother stared at him in amazement. "Thane, I can't tell you how surprised I am to see you doing so well."

Her father's response was more sobering, however. "I can tell you right now, you will never return to what you once were, but you can create a new standard for normal."

Thane nodded. "Wise words. Thank you for the honest insight, Dad."

Rytsar saw Brie smile. Thane's use of the familial title instantly lessened the tension in the room. The man was a genius.

His leg muscles were trembling from the effort of standing, so the two men helped him back onto the bed. "If you don't mind, I need a few minutes to speak with my parents."

"Of course, Mr. Davis," James replied, and the two men quickly left the room.

Rytsar went to follow them, but Thane asked that he stay. He nodded and moved closer to Thane, intrigued by his comrade's ability to take the unexpected situation in hand.

"Brie tells me she kept you both at arm's length after

the crash."

Bill gave Brie a side-ways glance and replied irritably, "She did."

"I want to assure you that will not be the case now."

Marcy's face lit up. "I was just telling Brie I would be happy to help in any way I can. I'm completely at your disposal."

Thane smiled at her. "I wish we could have you stay with us but, as you can see, our apartment is bursting at the seams at the moment. However, if you're willing to assist with errands, it would be a significant help to Brie and I. It would be even more important to me if you could take your daughter out and give her time away from this place. She has been a devoted wife and care-giver almost to a fault and could seriously use a little 'me' time."

"Of course, Thane. It would be my joy." Marcy looked at her daughter lovingly.

Brie, on the other hand, looked at Sir with a sad expression. "But I don't want to leave your side, Sir."

"Babygirl, you have been at my side for how many months? It's important that you take time for yourself and enjoy these last months of pregnancy."

"Oh, honey," her mother exclaimed, "I would love to go shopping with you for some stylish maternity clothes."

"I would like to spend time talking to my daughter alone. I'm tired of the silent treatment you've subjected us to."

Brie looked at Thane warily.

He responded with a gentle smile. "I would love to

see my beautiful wife dress up for a change. Show off your baby bump with pride, my dear."

Brie returned his smile but sighed heavily, obviously still struggling with the idea of leaving Thane after caring for him for so long.

"Why are you reluctant?" Bill demanded.

Rytsar spoke up when Brie was slow to answer. "I believe your daughter has been so busy caring for everyone else that she's forgotten what it is like to be cared for. It will do her good to spend time with the people who raised her."

Marcy put her arm around her daughter's shoulder. "Hon, remember when we went shopping for your wedding dress? Think of all the laughing we did, and now it's going to be for maternity clothes." She shook her head, smiling. "I can't believe my little girl is having a baby."

Brie gazed at her mom as if remembering that time and smiled. "It would be nice to shop together."

"So it's settled, then. What errands would you like us to run?"

Thane gestured to Rytsar. "My friend, Durov, is taking care of the logistics for me."

Bill frowned, apparently displeased to be working with the man who had goaded him at the wedding.

Rytsar understood his resistance after the entertaining razzing he'd given the man at Brie's wedding breakfast. He knew if he were going to be an exceptional *dyadya*, he had to be in good standing with *moye solntse's* grandparents. It was a requirement of the job.

Putting his right hand on his chest, he told Brie's father, "Mr. Bennett, I know I made a bad impression when we met last. I am heartily sorry for provoking you unnecessarily. As Brie's father and Thane's father-in-law, you deserve only my utmost respect."

"Now you're trying to pull my leg," Bill growled angrily.

Rytsar looked crushed. "I assure you I'm not. While I will admit I enjoy giving a good ribbing, it was not my place—especially with you."

Bill shook his head. "Why do I get the impression you're just baiting me so you can laugh at me later?"

Rytsar looked to Brie in exasperation, uncertain how he could win the man over, but still determined to try. "Mr. Bennett, if you have any cause to doubt my sincerity in the future, please call me on it."

Marcy reached out and stroked her husband's arm. "Dear, I believe the man is being sincere. Accept his apology."

Bill looked Rytsar up and down with a critical eye. "What you've been through, I can only imagine, based solely on how you look. I trust it made you take life more seriously, and is the only reason I am giving you the benefit of the doubt right now. But, be aware, I don't give second chances."

Success!

Rytsar gladly accepted her father's terms and winked at Brie when Bill wasn't looking. While he would absolutely show the man the respect he deserved, it didn't mean he might not have a little fun with the guy every now and then.

He had to remain true to himself, after all.

Rytsar took Mrs. Bennett's hand and kissed it gently. "I will leave you to speak with your son alone while I come up with a list of things you can do to help."

Her mother blushed. "That would be lovely." Her blush reminded him of Brie for a moment and made him smile.

Rytsar left the room feeling good about the overall outcome.

But there was a dark cloud still hanging over Brie's happiness. The beast named Lilly remained a serious threat to Brie. He'd heard of Wallace's plans for the women, and while both Thane and Brie supported them, he had little hope that Lilly would be swayed by anything she experienced there.

Some people were unsympathetic and needed the fear of God put in them.

Legacy

Knowing what needed to be done, Rytsar contacted the man Wallace had hired to pursue and capture Lilly once she escaped from jail. Rather than speak over the phone, Rytsar met up with Nick in person at a nearby park where they could speak in private.

"Wallace said you have been hired to capture her once she escapes from jail, after the birth of the child."

The man's eyes shone with anticipation. "And it should be any day now. I've heard rumors from the prison nurses that she's just been transferred to a different ward in the prison, a sure sign the baby is coming. I've already had a location device inserted under her skin during one of her recent examinations. We can track her down by sending radio signals to the implant."

"Excellent." Rytsar was extremely pleased by the man's thoroughness.

They spoke at great length about the logistics and timing of how he would ensnare and eventually capture her after a prolonged and carefully orchestrated chase.

"I only see one flaw."

"What's that?" Nick asked, sounding honestly interested.

"I am not a part of it."

"I'm positive we are adequately staffed for the operation," he replied.

"You are, and I have no interest in interfering, only adding to Lilly's experience during the hunt. You see, she is familiar with me. If she sees I've returned and am in pursuit of her, we will inspire the level of fear that Wallace hoped for."

Nick smiled at his suggestion. "I like the idea, Rytsar, but let me make a quick call to Mr. Wallace before I agree to anything."

Rytsar approved of the man's loyalty to Wallace, even though it was Rytsar who was footing the bill. The fact that the man wasn't swayed by that proved he was someone to be trusted.

While waiting for Nick to okay it with Wallace, Rytsar thought about Lilly—the woman who had not only framed her own sibling in a paternity suit, but had gone so far as to drug Brie in an attempt to kidnap her with the intention of killing the baby and selling Brie to the highest bidder. There could be no mercy shown to someone as ruthless and cunning as that.

When Nick ended the call, he let Rytsar know that Wallace was on board with having him join in the procurement of Lilly.

"Good. I cannot tell you how deeply I loathe this woman, and I'm sure she feels the same about me—but for vastly different reasons."

"Do you plan to be the one to actually apprehend her?"

"No, that will be the best part. I will be chasing her while you chase her, steering her like a pack of wolves toward the final destination, where you will abduct her. I strongly suggest you throw a hood over her head and take her on a long car ride. We'll add a plane ride to the mix before you bring her back to LA. She will have no way of knowing where she is, and the fact that I am not her captor means she will be living in constant fear, wondering when I will come and make my final strike."

"I like the devious way you think."

"When it comes to protecting those I love, I know no limits," Rytsar answered. "I am counting on you to call me the minute you get the word she's in active labor so we can begin our game of cat and mouse."

Nick held out his hand to Rytsar, and he shook it. "I look forward to working together."

The next order of business was visiting Stephanie Conner, the woman in charge of the center where Lilly was to spend her incarceration. Stephanie was the girl he'd rescued in Russia while Brie was visiting him at the cabin. The same girl who'd indirectly caused the kidnapping and torture he'd suffered at the hands of the Koslovs for killing the maggot who'd abducted her.

Rytsar had avoided all contact with her once he received Stephanie's letter shortly after her rescue. In it, she'd expressed how lost she'd felt. Stephanie's words had frightened him because they were too similar to

Tatianna's thoughts just before she'd ended her own life.

Rather than chance a meeting with her, and possibly making the situation worse, Rytsar had hired a string of counselors who specialized in survivors of human trafficking until she found one she worked well with.

When that counselor had informed Rytsar that Stephanie needed a positive outlet for her grief and depression, Rytsar thought back to what had given him satisfaction while grieving for Tatianna. It was in helping other girls escape the same hell that he'd found a purpose. But it was always with the silent hope that these girls would go on to live normal lives, since Tatianna could not.

Rytsar needed Stephanie to survive, so he'd invested in a large center north of LA that would act as a safe house for victims of sexual slavery. It would not only provide a protected environment, but also the counseling, physical care, and sense of community these survivors required to move forward.

After he'd gotten everything in place, he'd sent his only letter to her.

Dear Miss Conner,

I know it has been quite some time since you sent your letter to me. Every word you penned has been etched in my mind, and I have worked tirelessly to give you something of worth to match the courage you have shown.

I told you once that you were never a puppet, only a survivor. Survival takes bravery and tenacity. It is a fight, and you are my champion.

You mentioned in the letter that you wished you could repay me. Your success is your payment and, to that end, I have created something with you in mind.

When you said that you felt only I could understand what you had been through, I empathized with you. It is true that only those who have experienced such horrors firsthand have any knowledge of the hardships and abuses you faced.

Sadly, there are many who have had to walk in your shoes since you returned home. Like you, they feel alone and lost.

This is why I funded the Tatianna Legacy Center to help survivors like you. I have brought the best staff and resources together in one place so that no one has to be left behind to struggle alone after escaping the horrors of sexual slavery.

I am pleased to present this to you as my belated answer to your letter. I'm also offering you a chance to run it. Who better to oversee things than a survivor herself?

I have support staff who are at your disposal. It is my hope that you will find the satisfaction in helping others that I have found in helping you.

You are not alone. I will always be your unseen supporter.

Sincerely,
Rytsar Durov

Stephanie had responded with reservation, afraid she would not be up to the task of running the center. However, once she had met the girls she would be helping, Stephanie jumped in feet first and never looked back.

It did his heart good knowing that not only had Stephanie jumped the hurdle that Tatianna had been unable to but also, through her experiences, she was helping others do the same.

He wanted to share the joy of her success, so he asked Brie to accompany him.

"Of course, I would love to go," Brie told him. "Both Sir and I have been curious about how Stephanie's been doing, as well as the center you created, ever since Faelan mentioned it to us."

"Why is it that you have never spoken of it, brother?" Thane asked him.

Rytsar grinned when he answered. "If I'm to remain mysterious and alluring, I cannot be an open book, even to you."

Thane smirked. "I'll remember that."

"*Radost moya*, part of the reason I would like you to join me is to make certain that Stephanie sees me simply as a hands-off benefactor. I have no designs on her and never will."

"Not like Mr. Holloway," Brie replied with distaste.

"Your producer?" Rytsar punched his fist into his hand. "What has he done to you?"

Brie grabbed his wrist and forced it back down to his side. "It's not me, it's Mary. He's got something going on with her that caused the breakup with Faelan. The man is being shady about it too. I don't trust him."

"So does Wallace need me to set him straight?" Rytsar growled, punching his hand again.

"No, old friend. Wallace is handling things on his own. No need to get involved," Sir cautioned him.

"But I owe the kid, *moy droog*. If there ever comes a time, I will see to it that the situation is taken care of in a satisfactory manner."

"So long as you've spoken to Wallace beforehand."

"I would never do anything without Wallace's consent." He paused for a moment, then smirked at Thane. "Unless I don't agree."

"Tell me, Rytsar, how long has it been since you've seen Stephanie?" Brie asked.

"I have not seen her since that night, *radost moya*."

"The night that you rescued her?" she asked, surprised.

He nodded. "I have kept up with her through my contacts ever since she returned to America. I have a vested interest in Stephanie's survival."

"I know you do." Brie wrapped her arm around him, knowing how deeply he still suffered from the loss of Tatianna. "It must make you proud to see how far Stephanie's come."

"My pride had no place in this."

"Maybe I misspoke," Brie amended. "I simply meant that you must be grateful to see what she's accomplished."

He kissed her on the head. "*Da*."

The center was north of LA, nestled near Topanga State Park, an area that offered the tranquility of nature with the convenience of an active city and beach nearby.

"Rytsar…this is wondrous," Brie said, tears coming to her eyes as they pulled up. "The Tatianna Legacy Center. I can't think of a better name. And this location—I had no idea there were scenic hiking trails so close to LA."

"I think it does nicely," he replied, pleased by her response.

Rytsar led Brie into the building, and they were greeted by the sounds of trickling water from an indoor fountain, along with an abundance of live plants lining the walls of the room. That hadn't been in his initial plans, but he approved of the change.

He took it all in as he walked up to the receptionist, who stood up as he approached.

"Mr. Durov, what a pleasant surprise."

Brie whispered, "What? You didn't tell them we were coming?"

"What better way to find out how things are running than to come unexpected?" he answered under his breath as he smiled at the woman.

"Can you let Miss Conner know we are here?" he asked, turning to introduce Brie. "This is Brie Davis, my…" He paused for a moment, unsure of what to say.

Brie held out her hand to the receptionist. "Yes, I'm Brie Davis, Rytsar's joy." She grinned as she glanced at him.

Rytsar chuckled, smirking at her answer.

"Excuse me while I let Miss Conner know you both are here."

Rytsar watched as the woman left the room, entering a door on the left.

"You've created quite a place here, Rytsar," Brie exclaimed. "It feels serene just walking into the building. I'm sure it must make the new patients feel comfortable when they first enter here.

He looked around the large space. "This isn't my doing."

"No, it isn't. However, I hope you approve, Rytsar Durov. I added those elements for the very reason Mrs. Davis just stated."

He turned around to greet Stephanie, but the girl was hardly recognizable. Before him stood a seasoned businesswoman. Someone glowing with health and vitality.

"I most definitely approve, Miss Conner."

She blushed at his compliment. "I…I can't believe you are standing here in front of me. I was deathly afraid I would never see you after watching that footage on the news."

Rytsar cleared his throat. "Fortune is kind to the foolish."

Stephanie took his hand and shook it vigorously. "It's good to see that karma rewards heroes."

"Not a hero," Rytsar corrected.

She looked at Brie, smiling. "Well, I'm not sure what you call a man who saves your life, makes sure you are taken care of, and gives you a center like this to assist others."

"There is no doubt that Rytsar is an exceptional man. However, I also know he speaks highly of you. If you are going to use hero to describe him, then you would have to use it to describe yourself, as well."

Stephanie blushed a deeper shade of red and glanced at Rytsar. "Okay, the word 'hero' is a bit uncomfortable to bear. Let me just say I admire you deeply and am grateful for the influence you've had on my life."

Rytsar nodded. "I feel the same toward you, Miss Conner."

She smiled at them both. "Would you like me to show you around the place? There are some restricted areas to preserve our girls' privacy, but I'd be happy to share what we do here on a daily basis."

"That would be lovely," Brie said, linking her arm through Rytsar's.

"And while we walk, we can discuss the other matter Mr. Wallace came to me about."

"Certainly," Rytsar agreed. "However, I would prefer we discuss that after the tour, in private."

"Of course," Stephanie replied, blushing again.

Rytsar observed her the entire tour. Her confidence and passion for the center, and her deep-seated belief in the difference it was making to those she served, was thrilling to witness. This was not the broken girl he'd rescued from the maggot. This was a fully realized woman who was just beginning on her future path.

"How many survivors have graduated from your program?" Brie asked.

"I'm not sure if you are aware, Mrs. Davis, but the average life expectancy of a girl taken and sold into slavery is less than seven years. They normally die of AIDS, homicide, or suicide. Not enough make it to our doors. But I am proud to say that of those who do, we hold a 98 percent graduation rate, with only a few finding it necessary to return once leaving our program. With proper medical treatment, counseling, and the extensive rehabilitation services the center offers, we are truly a community of survivors."

Rytsar closed his eyes for a moment. *Do you hear that, my little sparrow? Stephanie is well, and she is helping countless others. You live on through me and all the survivors here.*

He had to hold back the tears that wanted to escape.

At the end of the tour, Stephanie led them to a private meeting room and asked one of her assistants to supply them with coffee and water before leaving them undisturbed.

"So, about the girl you want us to keep," Stephanie began.

Rytsar narrowed his eyes. "I do not think of Lilly as a girl, but a menace to society. No different than the maggot I killed the night I rescued you."

Stephanie inclined her head to him in acknowledgement.

"Miss Conner, it is hard for me to even talk about her. Lilly wanted to kill my baby," Brie explained, clutching her belly. "And she also planned to sell me into the very slavery your girls have been freed from. If I hadn't been rescued by Tono Nosaka, I would not be talking to you now. I have zero sympathy for the woman."

"Mr. Wallace informed me of the severity of her crimes against you, which is why I am determined to help." She turned to Rytsar. "I would do anything for you."

"While I appreciate the sentiment, Miss Conner, there is no need to feel obligated. I hope I made that clear in my letter to you," Rytsar stated.

Stephanie nodded, her eyes softening. "I understand where you are coming from. But no matter what you say, I will always feel indebted to you."

Rytsar shrugged, giving her a half-grin. "I suppose I can appreciate that, since there are many I am beholden to for my own recent liberation."

"I'm glad you understand," she said, sitting back in her chair and smiling at him. "I'm so very grateful to every person involved in your rescue. I don't know how I would have handled it if the outcome had been different." There was a flash of pain in her eyes before she glanced away.

Wanting to change the subject, Rytsar informed her, "I've been told that the birth is imminent. Are the two rooms ready?"

"They are."

Brie asked, "And are you confident she won't be able to get out and hurt me or anyone else here?"

"I assure you that all precautions have been taken, Mrs. Davis. But it was more than incarceration that Mr. Wallace spoke of. He talked about his wish to rehabilitate her and, after much thought, I think I have come up with a solution."

"Go on," Brie encouraged her.

Rytsar listened with interest, but still held the belief that rehabilitation was not possible with Lilly. For Brie's peace of mind, however, he was willing to give Wallace's plan a chance.

"As you know, she will be performing menial tasks under the watchful eye of your guards, to keep our facility running, but that isn't enough to rehabilitate a person."

"I completely agree," Brie told her.

"Therefore, I would like to utilize your informant. Since Lilly was essentially acting as a trafficker in her plans for you, Mrs. Davis, she should know what it entails from the victim's point of view."

Stephanie turned her gaze back to Rytsar. "I thought it would be beneficial to have your informant listen to recordings of the girls' interviews detailing what they suffered at the hands of their captors. She can pass on what she hears as if she knows the girls personally and is simply sharing their stories.

"Of course, I will ask permission of my girls to use their recordings with the explanation that it will be utilized to help others. I would never compromise their trust. After what they've been through, trust is a very fragile thing."

Rytsar nodded his approval. "Although there are no guarantees this creature has a heart, I commend you for coming up with a solution in the spirit of what Wallace was hoping to achieve here."

He looked at Brie. "What do you think, *radost moya*?"

"I know jail time has not made a difference to her.

At least, with this approach, Lilly might gain some empathy for others. I hope it will have *some* impact, and with an informant keeping us up to date, at least we might get a clearer picture of what's going on in that crazy head of hers."

"Good," Stephanie said, standing up. A blush colored her cheeks when she asked Rytsar, "Would it be okay if I hugged you?"

The request caught him off guard. "Understand that I am still recovering from my injuries. But if you are gentle…"

Stephanie stepped up to him, barely touching his body as she wrapped her arms around his torso and laid her head lightly on his chest. "Thank you," she whispered.

He felt tears pricking his eyes, and put one arm around her. "Thank you for flourishing."

Rytsar pulled away, giving her a curt bow before placing his hand on the small of Brie's back and walking her out with a smile on his face.

Stephanie's survival and service to others who were like her would remain a pinnacle of his life. Proof that something positive could come out of a tragedy.

Big Guns

Rytsar watched a naked Brie pick up her fantasy journal and curl up on the couch to write. He smiled to himself. That fantasy journal's first entry would always remain a favorite of his.

He walked into Thane's room to find his friend working out his arms with elastic bands. The man was working hard enough to draw a serious sweat.

"Don't go killing yourself," Rytsar warned him.

"I'm not staying in this bed a minute longer than necessary." Thane stopped to flex his arm. "Do you see it?"

"What?"

"The definition of a muscle."

Rytsar moved in close to look and clicked his tongue. "If you say so, *moy droog*."

Thane punched him in the arm, which actually hurt Rytsar because of his broken ribs, and he unconsciously grimaced.

"I didn't hit you that hard. I'm not that strong yet," Thane chided him.

Rytsar stood up, shifting uncomfortably.

"It's the ribs, isn't it?"

"Ah…" Rytsar knew there was no point in denying it, so he sighed in frustration, admitting to Thane, "They do not seem to be healing like they should."

"Because you refuse to slow down and rest."

Rytsar rubbed his rib cage, frowning. "It is not in my nature, comrade."

"You need to see Dr. Hessen. Don't put it off any longer."

"I'm not keen on doctors."

"See her, and if you like what she has to say, great. If not, you walk away and spend the rest of your life grimacing whenever I barely touch you."

Rytsar huffed. "I could take you in a fight."

Thane shrugged. "No contest, but beating up an invalid is frowned upon."

Rytsar burst out laughing. "You are no invalid. I think you're faking it."

Thane joined in his laughter.

"What going on in there?" Brie called from the other room. "You're not supposed to be having that much fun without me."

Thane smirked at Rytsar. "So you'll speak with Dr. Hessen, then?"

"*Da*, I will set up an appointment."

"Good, because I'm not into pussy Russians."

Rytsar shook his head slowly, growling under his breath, "You're asking for it, *moy droog.*"

Thane flexed his arm again. "Go ahead, tough guy. Take your chances with these big guns."

"Big guns? Water pistols are more like it."

Thane huffed and went back to his arm exercises.

Rytsar looked toward the door and asked him, "Do you know what your little submissive is doing out there?"

"Not a clue."

"She's writing in her fantasy journal."

Thane stopped for a moment. "Is she?"

"I'm curious about what she is writing."

Thane stated huskily, "As am I." He called out to Brie. "Babygirl, when you are done with your fantasy, come here and read it to your Master."

The pitter-patter of her bare feet sounded in the hallway. She peeked in and smiled. "It would be my pleasure, Master, but it may be a while."

"Take as much time as you need."

She winked at them both before disappearing again.

"I enjoy your woman's creative mind," Rytsar complimented him.

"It was one of the reasons I fell in love with her."

Rytsar stared at the doorway. "Am I allowed to listen when she reads it to you?"

"If you make the appointment with Dr. Hessen before she comes back."

Rytsar shook his finger at him. "You are a crafty bastard."

While Rytsar was finishing his call, he noticed Brie

closing her journal. She then began to play with herself.

"Good fantasy?"

"Real nice," she purred, looking at him unashamedly.

"I love your dirty mind, *radost moya*."

Brie giggled as he walked with her down the hallway.

When they entered the room, he announced, "*Moy droog*, after much concentration and pussy wetting, your sub is ready to share her masterpiece."

Thane patted the area next to him on the bed. "Come here, babygirl. I have been anxious to hear your latest entry."

He looked at Rytsar and asked, "Did you make the appointment?"

"I did."

"Then you are welcome to stay with us."

"Wonderful, but I need to get something first."

Rytsar left their room to get his Magic Wand. He figured it would make Brie's reading of her journal entry much more enjoyable for them all.

When he returned with the instrument, Brie's eyes widened. "Oh, no…" she murmured, her lips upturned in a little grin.

Rytsar plugged it in and tossed the large vibrator to Thane. "Why don't you tease her with it while I read the journal to you both?"

Thane switched it on, and its familiar buzz filled the room, causing Brie to squirm beside him. He switched it back off and smiled. "An excellent suggestion."

Pushing himself to a higher upright position, Thane commanded, "Come téa, snuggle up against your Master while I listen to your masterpiece."

Brie giggled as she handed her journal to Rytsar before scooting closer to Thane and laying her head on his chest, sighing contentedly.

Rytsar reached out to pet her hair as he opened the journal to the marked page.

He cleared his throat for dramatic effect before beginning.

My Master is working in the bedroom with his physical therapist.

I've been told that today is going to be his graduation day from therapy. I'm thrilled because I know how hard he has worked, and getting to this day has been a long, hard battle.

I'm in the kitchen, icing the cake I've made especially for the occasion. The Russian and the beefy male nurse are in the main room, engaged in what appears to be an intense conversation.

The Russian breaks away and joins me in the kitchen just as I am making the final touches to my decorations.

"That is a mighty fine-looking cake, but how does it taste?" Without asking, he swipes his finger across the top to take a taste.

"You!" I cry, hastily trying to fix the fingerprint with my frosting knife.

"It is good," he tells me, swiping his finger a second time and placing a dollop of it on my nose. "You should taste it."

Before I can react, he licks it off and then kisses me.

The sweet taste of vanilla buttercream fills my mouth. I push him away, laughing as I do so, and go back to fixing the cake.

He leaves me as my Master slowly but steadily walks from the hallway to the main room without any assistance.

When he looks in my direction and winks, my heart melts.

I pick up my little cake and walk into the main room with

everyone else. "Happy Graduation Day!"

He looks down at my creation, marred by the Russian's tasting, and smiles at me. "I look forward to feeding it to you."

I blush.

He wraps one arm around me, leaning down for a kiss and, all at once, I am spirited away as I lose myself in the familiarity of his embrace. It has been a long time since he's kissed me while standing, and I am so overwhelmed that a tear escapes.

My Master pulls away, a mischievous look in his eye as he wipes away the stray tear.

"Before I feed you cake, I want to celebrate in another way."

The Russian takes the cake from me and sets it on the table while my Master guides me to his tantra chair.

My heart starts to race, but I remain silent, waiting to hear his orders.

Suddenly, my Master, the Russian, and the two brawny medical personnel begin undressing in front of me.

"Master?"

"As you have already surmised, today's celebration will involve you pleasing all four of us men at the same time."

I look at each man, my heart now beating a mile a minute.

I know my Master's body well and love the dark hair that covers his chest and thighs, and frames his handsome cock. Sir's shaft is perfect in every way, and it knows exactly how to please me.

The Russian is a solid and muscular man, his chest broad and his stomach ripped with muscles. He also sports a dragon tattoo on his shoulder that defines his spirit—fierce and fiery.

The physical therapist is muscular, as well. His sandy blond hair and clean-shaven face give him a distinctly Californian look. I imagine him on the beach while girls swoon over him as he steps out of the ocean, wet and dripping, his body glistening in the sunlight.

As for the nurse, he has a body that reminds me of Master Coen. A bodybuilder in physique, with muscles everywhere. Although he has a head of curly brown hair, the man is completely hairless everywhere else to show off those bulging muscles. I find it quite intriguing.

"Undress, téa," my Master commands.

I look at him as I begin to shed my clothes. I do it sensually, like a love letter to him, exposing each area of skin to his gaze slowly, building the anticipation.

Once fully naked, I stand before my Master in a pose of submission, my hands open, my lips supple, my head bowed, knowing that soon I will be touched by these four men.

My Master comes to me first and lifts my chin to kiss me on the lips. I moan in pleasure, captivated by his passionate kiss. When I feel his hand close around my throat as his tongue enters my mouth, my body gushes with a need for him.

I instinctively reach out and begin stroking his cock, the thickness of his shaft making my pussy ache with need.

That is when I feel the distinct pressure of teeth as the Russian bites my shoulder. His hands caress my buttocks lustfully, causing chills of pleasure.

Then the other two join in, touching my breasts, squeezing and gently tugging at my nipples as they explore my body for the first time.

I moan loudly, overwhelmed by the attention of four men.

My Master moves his hand between my legs and announces to the others, "She's exceptionally wet."

Suddenly, all four men are touching my pussy, wetting their hands with my excitement. Their masculine groans fill the room as they taste it, exciting me even more.

The sexual tension in the room increases as my Master tells the Russian to lie on the tantra chair and then orders me to mount him.

The other two men each take one of my arms and help me straddle him before lowering me onto his rigid cock. He grabs my waist to grind his cock deeper into me.

From behind, I hear the slippery sound of lubricant being applied, and I know what comes next.

The Russian pulls me down onto his chest so my ass is exposed.

My Master then straddles the tantra chair behind me, and I feel the electricity of his touch as he caresses me. "I have always loved this ass, babygirl."

I smile to myself, longing for him to possess it again with his cock.

He spreads my ass cheeks apart and admires me for a moment before pressing the head of his shaft against my anus. I hold my breath. My pussy is already full with the Russian's manhood, and I know his entrance will be challenging for me, but I crave it.

"Relax…" he growls huskily as he pushes into me.

I gasp as his shaft enters, even though I have been taken this way before. It is always a pleasant shock to my system having two men fuck me at the same time.

As they begin to move inside me, I cry out in rapture as my body adjusts to their girth and measured thrusts.

But my bliss is ramped up as the two men join us, standing on either side of me.

I greedily take their hard shafts in my hands and grasp firmly as I stroke them. I am like a kid in a candy store, every wish fulfilled as I begin sucking on a cock, my hand still wrapped around the other.

I am pleasuring four cocks at the same time—one buried deep inside my pussy, teasing my G-spot mercilessly, while another penetrates my ass, fucking me ever deeper and demanding more and more of me. All the while, my oral fixation is satisfied as I take a third cock in my mouth, sucking eagerly as I stroke the fourth enthusiastically. The sensation of taking so many shafts at once blows my submissive mind and I embrace the sheer joy of it.

I don't think it can get any better, but my Master isn't finished yet. I hear an odd sound reminding me of metal spurs, and suddenly I feel a double trail of tiny pricks along my back that send chills throughout my entire body.

I mumble with a cock still in my mouth, "What's that?"

My Master shows me, holding his hand in front of my eyes. I see that he has slipped a new tool over his index finger. On the end of this unusual instrument are two Wartenberg wheels.

I moan from the delightful sensation his new tool adds to the experience. He deepens his thrusts, keeping a slow but steady pace as he crisscrosses the wheels over my back.

My body is humming at the cusp of an orgasm and I beg, "May I come Master?"

"Yes, téa."

I cry out in pure ecstasy at his answer. My climax takes over, and I give in to it completely.

The men let out individual groans, which turns me on even more as they watch and feel the intensity of my orgasm.

Once over, my mind and body become deliciously numb.

"Good girl…" my Master murmurs, bringing joy to my heart.

He then informs me, "Now, prepare for us to return the favor."

I throw my head back as both the Russian and my Master grab onto my waist and begin concentrated thrusts. I am only momentarily distracted, and quickly return my attention to the other two cocks I have been charged with to pleasure. I alternate between the thick, veiny shaft of the nurse and the long, hairless one of the physical therapist, loving the power my lips have over them.

I revel in my role as the ultimate vessel of pleasure as the Russian comes first, closely followed by my Master, and then the nurse, whose cock is in my mouth. I swallow his come and quickly switch to take the therapist last, deepthroating him as he comes.

Afterward, I collapse against the Russian.

I am exhausted but flying high from the sensual experience as my Master gently runs his fingers over my back.

I am in bliss…

Rytsar finished the last sentence to the passionate cries of *radost moya* beside him.

He watched in amusement as her hips bucked when her climax claimed her.

Thane raised an eyebrow and held out the wand to him, now wet with her come.

Rytsar smirked as he took the vibrator and placed it back on her quivering pussy.

Oh, yes, he most definitely wanted to tease that naughty submissive for making him so damn horny with her words.

No mercy.

The Chase

Rytsar got the call from Nick at two in the morning. He immediately called Wallace to let him know he was headed out to the jail to await the birth and would be waiting there when Lilly made her first move.

"I'd like to join you," Wallace stated.

"But you have a job and other responsibilities," Rytsar said, not wanting to have his hands tied by Wallace's kinder demeanor.

"Just for a day. I will go crazy if I remain here."

Rytsar could understand his point, and agreed. "I'll pick you up on my way. Get ready, Todd. Lilly's reeducation is about to begin."

"Thank you, Anton. I appreciate it."

Rytsar quietly got dressed and snuck into Thane's room. He knew his friend was a light sleeper and simply touched him on the shoulder.

Thane instantly opened his eyes and turned his head toward Rytsar.

Rytsar put his finger to his lips. Making the sign for crazy, he then pointed toward the door and held up his bag to let Thane know he was leaving.

Thane nodded, glancing over at Brie.

Rytsar quietly walked out of the room with Brie none the wiser as she lay sleeping next to her Master. It made him glad to know she was safe, and he would do everything in his power to keep it that way.

Wallace was waiting outside of Marquis's house. For some reason, he had the dog with him.

Rytsar unrolled his window. "We are not taking *Mudryy* with us."

Wallace laughed as the canine jumped up on Rytsar's car door and began licking his face, bouncing up and down on her hind legs.

"I know we can't take the dog, but *Mudryy* would never forgive me if I did not allow her a chance to say hello to you. I'm certain she would have woken up the neighborhood, as well as Marquis and Celestia, with her barking."

Rytsar frowned at Wallace, saying doubtfully, "And you're certain she won't bark now?"

Wallace rubbed the top of the dog's head. "She's a real smart animal. I'm not only positive she would have known you were here even if I hadn't brought her out, but I'm just as positive she will go back in the house and wait patiently for our return."

Rytsar looked down at the dog, wagging her tail so excitedly her entire body was shaking back and forth from it.

Her joy in seeing him was too much. Unbuckling his seat belt, he opened the car door and got out to kneel next to her.

Mudryy went wild, trying to jump in his arms as she licked him all over.

Rytsar chuckled, quite won over by her obvious affection for him.

"I never knew a dog could be that intelligent," he said in wonder.

"Some are, but not all of them. Much like people."

Rytsar gave her one more all over body rub before he stood up and pointed toward the house.

Her ears fell and she whined softly but, when he pointed again, she dutifully followed Wallace back to the door and went in the house without protest.

Wallace came back smiling. "I told you, man. That dog is something else."

Rytsar nodded in agreement as he got in the car. He turned on the ignition, smiling to himself. He agreed with Wallace that the dog was special and, for some strange reason, *Mudryy* thought he was too.

"You won't have any issues when it comes time for me to take her back. Once Thane is healed up, and I'm not needed there twenty-four/seven, I plan on moving to my beach house, and thought the pup would like living there."

"I understand she's your dog. But, I won't lie. I'm going to miss her when you come to get her. Best companion I've had—ever."

"As long as we are on the same page," Rytsar said, staring at the road in front of him. "On that same note, I have something to ask you."

"Shoot."

"Brie mentioned that the producer Holloway has

been fucking with you."

"Fucking Mary is more like it," Wallace huffed.

"Do you need me to have a talk with this man?"

"Hell no," he immediately answered.

"Why not? It sounds like he deserves a punch in the face."

Wallace shook his head. "I have no idea what Holloway's deal is, but if Mary wants him, she can have him."

"You don't want your submissive back?"

Wallace snorted. "Mary was never my submissive. I may have thought she was, may have even gotten her to wear my collar, but that girl was a submissive unto herself."

"You're not man enough to punish her?"

"Mary lived for punishment. It was not a deterrent, believe me."

"What was it, then?"

Wallace sighed. "I think she wasn't ready, or I wasn't the right guy. I don't know, but there's no going back. She made her feelings very clear when she left. I may have a soft spot, and I do enjoy spoiling my subs, but try to emasculate me emotionally and I'm out. I may not be a sadist, but I'm definitely not a masochist. Humiliation can go fuck itself."

Rytsar burst out laughing. "You can say that again."

After the laughter died down, Wallace told him, "It really doesn't matter now, anyway. I've got something good going with Kylie. Although I'll admit I'm already in love with the girl, I am doing my damnedest to go slow this time. I'm not uttering those three words until I know beyond a shadow of a doubt that she feels the same about me."

"Wise."

Wallace shook his head, laughing at himself. "But, damn, it's hard."

"So you are good with Holloway?" Rytsar asked, wanting to confirm it.

"Hell no, I'm not good with him. I have no idea what the fuck he's up to, but I'm not going to do anything about it. That's Mary's problem now. She kicked me to the curbside."

Rytsar shrugged. "Does she need a talking to?"

Wallace grinned, patting Rytsar on the shoulder. "Look, you don't owe this guy nothing."

Rytsar nodded but did not reply.

"Hey, look, when you look at my eye, what's the first thing that goes through your head?"

"I remember how brave you were."

"Hmm…okay. What is the second thing you think, then?"

"I'm indebted to you."

Wallace snapped his fingers. "See, that's what I'm getting at. Listen to me, and listen good. You don't owe me a damn thing."

"But—"

Wallace shook his head. "Nope, not a Goddamn thing."

Rytsar gave him an exasperated look. "But the choice you made saved my life."

Wallace smiled, his face glowing with excitement. "Yes, it was *my* choice, and because of that, there is no obligation between us. You didn't beg me to do it. You didn't even ask me to do it. It was all on me. Nothing you could have said or done would have changed my decision. It was out of your hands." He sat back in his seat, letting out a self-satisfied sigh. "You only owe someone if you specifically ask them to help. And, even then, paying it forward is equally effective. Maybe even more so."

Rytsar shook his head. "You are a strange one, Todd. You work in a world of grays, while I see it all in black and white."

"I hold nothing against your perspective, Anton," Wallace assured him. "However, in the case of you and me, I'm right. From now on, when you look at my eye, what are you going to think?"

"That you are a stubborn dick."

Wallace smiled. "Fine. I can live with that."

Both Rytsar and Wallace were shocked that Lilly made her escape just two hours after the infant was born. While the nursing staff gave her privacy to see the child alone and say her goodbyes before the baby was taken from her, Lilly escaped.

Her breakout was quick and clean. Had they not been prepared, she would have disappeared without a trace.

Rytsar was reminded again of just how smart and conniving Lilly was. She was not someone to be toyed with or underestimated.

"Your man is handling the first one," Rytsar explained to Wallace.

Rytsar slowly drove the car, following behind Nick and his men.

It appeared that Lilly had someone waiting for her in a running vehicle. Just as she tried to head for the car, Nick's van pulled up and the side door swung open. Several hands tried to pull her in, but she struggled, and they let her break free.

Lilly ran, now aware that someone not only knew she had escaped, but had plans to take her.

Rytsar smiled at Wallace. "And the chase begins."

They spent the day keeping her on the move, never giving her time to rest or get her bearings. When she disappeared into an alley, Rytsar told Nick he wanted the opportunity to reintroduce himself.

Walking between the bricks buildings, a smirk on his face, Rytsar made his way to her. He could hear Lilly scavenging in a dumpster, but when she registered the sound of boots walking toward her, she suddenly stopped moving.

Rytsar stood there, patiently waiting, letting the time drag out, knowing it was killing her.

When he heard movement again, he started to whistle a familiar tune…

You are my sunshine.

Lilly didn't hesitate for a second, crawling out of the dumpster, screaming her fool head off as she ran blindly from him.

She didn't even look back, she was so intent on escape.

Rytsar chuckled to himself as he returned to the car.

He looked at Wallace and grinned.

"You're enjoying this too much," Wallace said.

"I admit it. I feed off her terror. All I have to do is think about what she did to Thane and Brie and her plans for the babe."

He nodded in understanding.

"So, are you ready to continue?"

"Of course," Wallace answered. "There's no other way to for this woman to comprehend what she's done unless she experiences it herself. It's like a toddler who bites, but can't understand that it hurts until he gets bitten himself."

Rytsar agreed and was grateful that Wallace was willing to let this play out. Lilly had to experience the heart-stopping terror she'd subjected Brie to—and she had to be subjected to it multiple times.

He didn't return to Thane's apartment for thirty-six hours. He planned to rest a few hours before heading back out, and he wanted to check in with Brie and Thane.

To his surprise, Brie's parents were already there, and the apartment was filled with the aroma of bacon and eggs.

"Mr. Durov, you're just in time!" Marcy announced when he walked in.

"For what?"

"We're flying out later this morning, so Bill and I wanted to share a last meal with everyone."

Bill was reading the newspaper on the couch and looked up briefly, nodding to him.

"Where's Brie?"

"I told her to dress in one of the outfits we bought."

Brie came out of the bedroom dressed in a fashionable black skirt and a top that showed off her growing breasts and stomach. He raised an eyebrow, liking the look very much.

"Good morning, Mrs. Davis," he said, choosing not to whistle out of respect for her parents.

When she saw Rytsar, Brie ran and hugged him. "You're back!"

"Back from what?" her father asked, putting down his newspaper.

"I have procured temporary employment. It requires long hours, but the payoff is great."

"You mean pay?" Bill corrected him.

Rytsar smiled in answer.

"Please, you two, sit down while I take this plate to Thane," Marcy told them.

Rytsar looked down at the plate heaped with scrambled eggs, bacon, and hash browns. Ironically, there was a thinly sliced tomato on the plate and he knew how much Thane hated tomatoes.

She noticed him staring at it and smiled. "Brie says he normally eats a healthy breakfast, so I added the tomato."

"Yeah," Bill said as he walked past them to the

kitchen table, "We don't believe in eating rabbit food for the first meal of the day where we come from."

"Neither do I, Mr. Bennett," Rytsar agreed heartily.

He sat down beside Brie and planned on waiting for her mother to return, but her father told him, "Dish up. Marcy hates it when the eggs get cold."

It looked as if she'd cook at least a dozen eggs, and Rytsar was starving. He heaped pile after pile on his plate.

"Leave some for the rest of us," Bill complained.

Marcy walked back just as Rytsar was about to put some back. "Oh, no. Please, Mr. Durov, I'll cook some more. It won't take me but a minute."

Rytsar smiled sheepishly at Bill, but then grabbed a handful of bacon off the serving plate.

When Bill growled in disapproval, Rytsar put one piece back, grinning at Brie.

"Mrs. Bennett, I love an All-American breakfast."

"Funny, that's just what Thane said a minute ago." She looked at Brie. "Honey, don't you start these men off with a good breakfast?"

Brie had a half-smile on her face, trying not to laugh.

"What's so funny, Brianna?" her father demanded.

"I made Sir a breakfast similar to this the first morning we were together."

"And?"

"He refused to eat it."

Her father shook his head, chuckling. "You never were much of a cook. Took after me."

"I'm sure you've gotten much better since then," Marcy exclaimed, putting a fresh pile of eggs on the serving plate. "Your husband was so sweet just now, telling me that the tomato was the perfect complement to the meal."

Brie stuffed her mouth with eggs, trying not to laugh.

Rytsar told her mother, "Sometime I will have to share with you a traditional Russian breakfast."

Marcy sat down and served herself, asking him, "What do you typically eat in Russia?"

"I enjoy a stack of *syrniki*, buttered bread with a thick slice of *kolbasa,* and a shot of vodka to start off my day."

Marcy smiled. "Sounds interesting, Mr. Durov."

Bill looked at him critically. "You drink in the morning?"

"I jest," Rytsar grinned, spooning another helping of eggs.

Brie smiled at her father. "I'm glad you came, Daddy."

For the first time since their arrival, her father's expression softened. He paused for a moment and said, "I'm glad too, Brianna."

Brie got up and walked over to him, giving her father a hug.

Marcy smiled at Rytsar. "Isn't it amazing what a good breakfast can do?"

With a full stomach and three hours of sleep, Rytsar headed back out. He took pleasure in knowing that Lilly was hungry and exhausted.

He pulled his car up to the van and got out to speak with Nick.

"I can take it from here for the next couple of hours. Do what I did and get some rest." He looked in the direction of the garage that Lilly was taking refuge in. "How is she doing?"

Nick smiled. "We've kept her active. She's probably curled up in there trying to sleep."

"Good. It's time she had a nightmare."

"You good, then?"

"Absolutely."

"We'll meet you at the abandoned hotel when you give us the word."

Rytsar laughed. "It will be glorious."

He watched the van leave.

Locking his car, Rytsar started walking toward the garage. Glancing around the neighborhood, he noticed men and women scurrying off to work, oblivious to him and the evil so near them.

Rytsar quietly entered through the side door and looked around the dark garage, giving himself time to let his eyes adjust. He could hear her steady breathing. It let him know she was sound asleep.

He took off his boots and placed them next to the door before moving quietly toward the sound.

Rytsar found Lilly curled up in a corner of the garage, huddled between mechanic tools and a stack of tires. Her hair was still short, but her fingernails had grown since he had last seen her. He'd have Nick take care of that.

It looked like she was suffering from a bad dream,

because her eyes kept darting back and forth wildly.

He just stared at her, not in any hurry.

Rytsar knew that her body was on high alert and sensed his presence. It wouldn't be long before her brain signaled her to open her eyes and she realized the danger she was in.

He purposely stood to the left so she would have a path to escape. The entire day would be devoted to her running from him.

There was no rest for the wicked—literally.

Lilly's eyes fluttered open. For a moment, she didn't move, then she turned her head and her mouth opened in a silent scream.

"Welcome to your nightmare."

She threw a terrified glance at the door. When he started toward her, she scrambled to her feet and ran.

Rytsar walked over to collect his boots, putting them on slowly. He then wiped his fingerprints off the handle of the door before leaving. There was no need to hurry since he could track her.

Like a true nightmare, he would keep coming for her.

The next time they met up, Lilly had laid in wait for him, wanting to smash him with a baseball bat she'd stolen along the way. He easily grabbed it from her and stared at the beast, bouncing the end of it against his palm.

"Where do you want me to hit you first?"

A group of joggers ran past, giving Lilly an audience. She screamed, getting their attention before she turned and ran.

Rytsar didn't move as they approached.

"What's going on here?" one of them asked, looking at the bat in his hand.

Rytsar laughed. "I have no idea. That crazy woman tried to hit me with it, and when I tried to stop her, she screamed and ran."

The men looked at him doubtfully as they surrounded him.

"He's telling the truth," a withered old man said, limping up to the group. "I saw it all from my porch." He looked at Rytsar excitedly. "She was waiting for someone to happen by like a black widow waiting for a fly."

The men's anger toward Rytsar suddenly shifted to one of concern.

"We better call the cops," one of them said, pulling out his phone.

"Yes, we should," Rytsar agreed. As soon as their attention was directed elsewhere, he slipped away unseen and continued his pursuit.

Rytsar smiled to himself. Lilly had no idea that each time she ran, she was moving closer and closer to her extraction point.

Wiping his fingerprints off the bat, Rytsar slung it into a yard covered with children's toys, hoping someone would be able to get some use out of it.

As he started in the direction of the vacant motel, Rytsar chuckled.

She would run there, a convenient place to hide among the outcasts of society, hoping there would be safety in numbers.

He was obvious in his approach, wanting Lilly to

hear him as he checked each room as he went down the line. He wanted her to dread the sound of his footsteps as he drew closer, and to experience the terror when the mind realizes escape is impossible.

He'd known that feeling. Tatianna had known that feeling. Now the beast would know it.

Rytsar saw Nick standing by, ready to snatch her when she ran.

Slowly opening the door, he heard the frightened whimpers of several of LA's homeless huddled together. The stench of human bodies and feces filled the room. A perfect place for Lilly.

He walked over to a soiled sleeping bag that seemed to have been thrown carelessly into the corner. His lips twitched as he walked over to it. He took a corner of it and lifted it up slowly.

"Boo."

Lilly screeched, looking to the others for help.

No one moved.

Understanding there was no rescue to be had, she started for the window. Rytsar was right behind her, grabbing at her as she dove headfirst through the broken window.

Rytsar stood next to the window frame and watched as she made a beeline across the parking lot. The white van sped towards her, blocking her path. Before she could react, the door swung open and she was dragged inside, kicking and screaming, just before it sped away.

He nodded, pleased.

Turning toward the huddled group, Rytsar walked up to them.

"Please don't hurt us."

Digging into his pocket, he pulled out his wallet and handed them all the cash he had. "Find a way home."

Rytsar met Wallace at the center the next night. Lilly's extended travel was coming to an end, and her reeducation would formally begin.

"I'm relieved things went so well," Wallace confessed as they waited.

Rytsar shrugged. "As long as you know what you are doing, and have the right people in place, it is never a problem."

Wallace smirked.

"Where is your informant?"

"She'll be here any moment."

"She understands what she must do?"

"Without question."

Rytsar furrowed his brow. "Who is she?"

Wallace pointed to a car pulling up. "That's her now. I'll let her introduce herself."

Rytsar watched with interest as the car pulled up and the lights were turned off. He was shocked to see Mary Wilson, the long-legged blonde, exit the car.

"Miss Wilson," he stated as she walked up.

"Rytsar?" she said in surprise, obviously shocked to see him.

She turned her gazed to Wallace and stopped mid-step, crying, "Faelan, what happened to *you*?"

He frowned. "It doesn't matter."

Mary rushed to him. "Doesn't matter? Don't tell me it doesn't matter. Just look at you…" She stared at his eye patch in horror.

"I'm fine," he insisted.

"You're not fine. Oh, my God, your beautiful face," she whimpered, tears coming to her eyes.

Wallace stepped back from her. "I don't need pity."

Rytsar spoke up. "Miss Wilson, you never mourn the battle scars of a hero."

Mary looked Rytsar over, seeming to notice for the first time the terrible condition he was in, as well.

Her face turned white, the blood draining from it, as she turned back to Wallace. "You almost died, didn't you?"

Wallace said nothing.

"He is a hero," Rytsar repeated firmly.

Mary looked at Wallace, shaking her head in disbelief. "Baby…is there anything I can do for you?"

"First, don't ever call me baby again, or Faelan, or any name other than Wallace," he replied.

She seemed hurt by his words, but asked him, "What else do you want me to do?"

"Do the job you came here to do. That's *all* I need from you."

"But, Fae—" She paused, stopping herself. Tears ran down her cheeks as she cried, "I almost lost you."

He snorted, shaking his head. "Let's focus on the task at hand. It's the only thing that's relevant."

"Do you know what you need to do, Miss Wilson?" Rytsar demanded.

She dragged her gaze from Wallace to meet his. "Yes, I understand perfectly."

"Good. I think it's best if you go to your room now and get comfortable. Lilly will be arriving in fifteen minutes."

Mary glanced back at Wallace, an unmistakable look of grief on her face.

"Now, Miss Wilson," Rytsar ordered.

She left them standing there in silence.

Once she was inside, Rytsar turned on him. "Why on earth did you pick her?"

Wallace answered confidently, "She's the best person for the job. I wasn't about to let our past history compromise Brie's safety. Mary can be ruthless, so she will understand Lilly, but she is also fiercely loyal to Brie. There is no other person I would trust to do this."

"How do you intend to make your working relationship function?"

"It's simple. She'll report to you. There will be no further need for us to communicate."

Rytsar sighed. "I don't care for this complication."

"It's only a complication if we make it one. I don't intend to."

"Who else knows about Mary?" Rytsar asked.

"Just Stephanie and a few of the staff who need to be involved. Keeping her identity secret is of utmost importance. She's taking a huge risk to help Brie."

Rytsar nodded. "*Da*, she is."

"Here they come," Wallace announced, looking at his watch as the vehicle approached. "It looks like they're a few minutes early."

Both Rytsar and Wallace stood in silence as the van

stopped and a hooded Lilly was dragged out of the van.

Rytsar could smell the fear on her, and smiled.

She was marched past them, having no idea they were watching. They followed the men inside and walked down to the basement to watch as she was led into the room. A heavy collar was placed around her neck and locked with a key. It was attached to a short chain, allowing for minimal movement. She would be kept chained except for the times she was allowed out to work.

"Where am I? What do you want from me?" she cried.

When the men didn't answer her, she resorted to bribes, then threats. But as they headed for the door, Lilly begged piteously, "Have mercy! Please, have mercy on me. I'm an American."

It disgusted Rytsar that she felt she deserved any mercy when she had so callously sentenced Brie to far worse.

The door was shut and the line of locks slid into place. There was no possibility of escape. Lilly would either be changed by this place or become lost in the prison of her own hellish mind.

Rytsar allowed everyone else to leave while he stayed behind.

After the halls had quieted down and Lilly stopped screaming, Mary's quiet voice, tinged with a Middle Eastern accent, hesitantly called out from the other side of the wall. "New girl…can you hear me?"

Rytsar smiled.

A new set of games had begun.

Mos-*cow*

Rytsar returned to Thane's apartment, exhausted but extremely satisfied. He was lusting for a long, uninterrupted sleep.

But as the elevator door opened to Thane's floor, he swore he heard the sounds of a party coming from their apartment. As he was attempting to unlock the door, it opened up and he was startled to find Lea standing before him.

"What are you doing here?"

"I've been begging to visit Brie for weeks now, and Thane finally gave me the okay."

She stepped aside to let him enter.

Rytsar felt a mix of emotions, seeing Lea again. He walked past her to see a very happy Brie.

"Can you believe she came for a quick visit?"

"A welcomed distraction," Thane said from the couch, sitting there dressed in a suit. Rytsar felt a surge of elation seeing his comrade looking like his old self. Even though he knew Thane still could not walk without assistance, this illusion was most welcomed.

"I must say, Rytsar, you're looking ruggedly handsome these days," Lea told him, pressing her impressive breasts against his chest as she hugged him.

"You mean royally jacked up," he corrected.

"Oh, no, a man with battle wounds is always sexy, in my book," she replied with a flirtatious smile. She turned to Brie and said, "I saved a Russian joke just for this moment."

Brie groaned, shaking her head but smiling at her friend just the same.

Lea turned to Thane and asked, "Where do Russians get their milk?"

Looking at Rytsar, she smiled brightly and answered, "From a Mos-*cow*."

Lea burst out in peals of laughter.

Brie bumped her hip. "Yep, that is one of the worst ones yet."

"What do you think of my little joke, Rytsar?" Lea asked.

"You know how I feel about your jokes, *mishka*."

"You love them so much you can't get enough?"

"*Nyet*."

She stuck out her bottom lip. "Really?"

"Is there any reason you would feel uncomfortable with me right now?" he asked her.

Lea's eyes grew wide, suddenly realizing that he knew. "I…I—"

Rytsar put his arm around her and turned Lea to face the other two, not wanting to mar this moment with a talk that should be taking place in private. "Let's celebrate this gathering of good friends."

Brie clapped her hands and grabbed Lea's wrist. "Do you want to feel the baby kick?"

Lea got a terrified look on her face, but closed her eyes and let Brie place her hand on her stomach. It only took a few moments before Lea's eyes popped open and she snatched her hand away.

"Oh, my gosh, that's so weird!"

"It's not weird. It's totally normal," Brie insisted.

Lea raised her eyebrows. "I'm sorry, girlfriend, but that's seriously freaky."

Thane spoke up. "Keep in mind, my dear, that Ms. Taylor hasn't seen you since the honeymoon. Your pregnancy has just been a concept in her head, not a reality."

"Sir Davis is right," Lea agreed. "But it's not only that. Feeling your stomach move like an alien's inside there is…"

Rytsar came over and placed his hand on Brie's stomach. The moment he felt *moye solntse* move, he grinned. "It's a beautiful miracle."

Lea gave him a half-grin. "Fine, it's a creepy but beautiful miracle."

They all sat down together as Brie and Thane shared the events that had occurred since the crash. Rytsar tried to listen, but his eyelids felt heavy, and he struggled to concentrate.

"It looks like you seriously need some sleep, Rytsar," Lea commented.

"I agree," Thane said. "If you don't mind, old friend, I need help to bed. Then you can retire and get the rest you need."

"Not a problem at all, comrade."

He helped Thane to his feet and took most of his weight as Thane leaned against him. The pain in his ribs was excruciating, but he bore it without complaint as Thane took slow steps back to the bedroom. Once he had his friend situated in bed, Rytsar bid them all goodnight and retired to his room.

As he was undressing, he heard a knock on his door.

"Rytsar?"

"Yes, Ms. Taylor."

"I know you're tired, but do you mind if we talk for just a minute?"

Naked, he slipped under the covers and told her, "You may come in."

Lea walked inside, shutting the door behind her. She moved over to the bed but sat on the corner near his feet.

"What is it?" he asked.

Her expression turned to one of concern and fear. "I've really tried to keep my cool tonight, but I've been sick with worry, completely terrified for you ever since you were abducted."

"Well, there was reason to be," he answered simply.

She picked at the material of the comforter nervously. "I know Mistress Clark went there to rescue you."

"She did," he answered coolly.

Lea met his gaze. "I assume she told you about the two of us."

"She did."

She bit her lip, looking at him nervously. "I'm sorry I didn't say anything. I wanted to, but…" Her voice trailed off and she became silent.

"I feel as if I was lied to," he replied.

Lea looked crushed but nodded. "I can understand why you might feel that way."

"There is no *might*," he told her.

"If you remember, I told you no, but you kept insisting."

"Had you said you and Ms. Clark were involved with each other, it would have ended right there."

"But I didn't want that to happen, Rytsar. Brie has always spoken so highly of you, so I wanted to scene with you. I know it sounds wrong, but if I had to do it again, I wouldn't change anything."

"You would lie again?" he asked, disappointed by her answer.

She looked at him sadly. "Yes, I would keep that fact from you so that we could scene together."

"So you are saying that you are not trustworthy."

"No, I'm not saying that at all."

"Then explain, because your character seems suspect to me."

She looked up at him, meeting his angry stare. "What happened that day was incredible. Not only as a kinky scene, but on an emotional level. I had no idea that would happen, and I've thought of little else since."

"You knew of the dark history between your Mistress and me. How could I not feel betrayed that you had kept that from me? I bared my soul to you."

"I never shared what we talked about with anyone. I would never betray your confidence."

His eyes narrowed. "But you did. Even after, you

could have come to me instead of letting me find out from the very person you were trying to hide from me."

Lea stood up, her entire body visibly trembling. "You're right. I should have told you. All I can do now is promise I will never lie to you again." She made a criss-cross sign over her heart, saying, "Cross my heart, hope to die."

Rytsar sighed. "I do not know how I feel about you now, and I am too tired to think about it further."

She bowed. "I understand. Thank you for letting me say my piece." She started toward the door, but turned around before she opened it.

"I don't have those panic attacks anymore." She smiled weakly as she walked out, quietly shutting the door.

As her footsteps grew fainter, Shadow appeared out from under the bed. He jumped on the dresser and sat, staring at Rytsar without blinking.

Rytsar chuckled, shaking his head as he leaned over to turn off the light on the nightstand. He laid his head back on the pillow and, before the covers even settled, he was asleep.

"You will need titanium plates if you want full motion again," Dr. Hessen told him. "Your ribs were not just broken, they were fractured in many places."

"You're suggesting an operation," he said, not liking the idea of going under the knife.

"Yes. We can screw titanium plates over each damaged rib."

Rytsar growled. "I don't trust doctors or hospitals."

Dr. Hessen smiled, not taking offense. "The stability will allow your ribs to heal quickly and, following surgery, you will not only be free of the pain, but you should be able to perform normal tasks within a few months."

"It sounds too good to be true."

She laughed. "My job is not to convince you of anything, but to let you know that you have this option. What you do with the information is up to you."

He looked at her skeptically. "You're not like any doctor I've ever met."

"What can I say, Mr. Durov? I believe knowledge is power. Fortunately for you, there is an effective solution."

Rytsar frowned. The idea of being put under general anesthesia actually terrified him. Pain he could handle, but not the total loss of control.

He stood up and shook her hand. "Thank you for your time, Doctor."

She smiled pleasantly. "I hope you found it helpful."

"You have given me much to consider."

Rytsar returned to the apartment and went directly to Thane. "Your doctor has messed with my head."

"How so?"

"She says I can be swinging my 'nines again in a couple of months."

"That's excellent."

"But it requires surgery."

"You'll recover quickly."

"I have an unnatural fear of going under the knife, *moy droog*. I am not sure I can do it."

Brie came into the room, smiling. "So did I hear right? Dr. Hessen can help?"

"Possibly, but it would require an operation and a stay at the hospital," Rytsar explained.

"How long for recovery?"

"She said five days before I could return home, and months before I felt like my old self."

"Only months? That's incredible!"

Rytsar nodded, still not convinced. "Almost sounds too good to be true."

Thane stared at him for a long time before asking, "Brother, what is it that concerns you about this?"

"I could be left in a vegetative state and be fed through a tube for the rest of my life."

"Seeing me like that upset you."

Rytsar gestured to him. "Looking at you now, it seems unreasonable. But, yes, I found it extremely disturbing, *moy droog*."

"So what are the chances of that happening?" Thane asked him.

"One in one hundred thousand."

"Those seem like good odds."

"Not to that one person. And then there is Lilly."

"Wallace can oversee that."

Rytsar clicked his tongue.

"In the end, this decision has to come from you, old friend."

"*Da*," he growled.

Brie came over and put her arms around him. "Just think, if you go through with the surgery, you'll be able to not only hold our little girl, but give her piggybacks or rides up on your shoulders when she's older."

His one kryptonite—the babe.

Rytsar looked at Brie's stomach, the decision already made.

"I will do it."

"And I can take care of you once you get out of the hospital," Brie offered.

"*Nyet*, your attention must remain on your Master."

Rytsar began pacing nervously, a flood of endorphins rushing through his veins as he confronted one of his greatest fears—and he accepted his fate.

"If I do this, I will move to my beach house and hire the best care so I can do what you are doing," he said, looking at Thane. "I will work myself relentlessly until I am fully recovered."

"We can spur each other on."

Rytsar gave him a curt nod. "It is settled, then. The sooner the better." He knelt, grasped Brie's belly, and spoke directly to the babe. "When we meet, I will dance with you without pain." When he looked up, he saw tears in Brie's eyes and knew with certainty that his decision was the right one.

"Thank you, *radost moya*."

"For what?"

"For reminding me where my priorities lie."

Her bottom lip trembled as she looked down at him.

Rytsar stood up and kissed those expressive lips. "It's not just *moye solntse* I wish to carry on my shoulder."

He looked at Thane. "We still have an isle date."

Thane smiled. "Yes, we do, old friend."

Thane insisted that Brie join Rytsar the day he moved his belongings into the beach house. There was a feeling of sadness, leaving their place behind. Brie sensed it too and it showed on her face.

"Do not be sad, *radost moya.* I will still be near."

"But I liked having you here every day. It won't seem the same without you."

"You need to return to the life you were building with my brother before the crash, and now I can be a part of it."

She nodded.

When he went to shut his suitcase, he found Shadow sitting in it on top of his clothes and burst out laughing. "I know you don't want to come with me, devil cat."

Shadow narrowed his eyes in answer.

Rytsar picked the animal up and set him on the bed. "While I will miss my nightly suffocations, I'm certain you will find *moy droog* an equally tempting target."

Shadow twitched his tail back and forth.

"You know where your duty lies, and soon there will be another for you to protect."

Shadow put up with the indignity of Rytsar patting him on the head as he headed out the door.

On the drive to the beach house, Rytsar informed Brie that he needed to make a short detour. When they pulled up to Marquis Gray's home, she grinned.

"Ah, you're here for the pup, aren't you?"

He'd already called Wallace to let him know they'd be coming. Although he knew the boy had grown attached to the animal, there was never any doubt who she truly belonged to.

It was made that much more evident as he approached the door and *Mudryy* started barking on the other side.

He grinned at Brie. "She already knows I'm here."

"I can't wait to meet her," Brie said excitedly.

The moment the door opened, the dog was on him, licking his face as she danced on her hind legs. He went down on one knee and let her have her affectionate way with him.

"Oh, Rytsar, she's adorable."

Wallace stood at the door, smiling down at the animal. "Smartest dog I've ever met."

Rytsar looked up and informed him, "We aren't here for a visit."

"That's fine. Marquis and Celestia aren't here, anyway. If you follow me to my room, I can give you all her stuff."

They walked down the hallway, the whole time *Mudryy* making it difficult to walk as she wiggled around him.

"She really likes you," Brie commented.

Rytsar shrugged. "What can I say? She has exceptional taste in men."

Wallace had a large basket filled with items, and a bag of dog food.

He smirked at Rytsar. "But, wait, there's more."

Mudryy was wagging her tail wildly, staring up at Rytsar with a look of expectancy.

"You know how Marquis mentioned that she steals from their table? She also haunts Celestia in the kitchen, looking for anything she might get her teeth into and sneak out with."

"Is it possible she believes she's still starving?" Rytsar asked, looking down at the mutt in concern.

"No." Wallace pulled back the cover of his bed and pointed.

When Rytsar moved closer, *Mudryy* raced under and came back with a stale dinner roll in her mouth, wagging her tail vigorously.

"She's been hoarding food for you. I've been having a heck of a time keeping it clean under there, but I've allowed her to keep an odd roll or two so she doesn't feel her efforts are wasted."

Rytsar looked at the dog, his heart bursting with overwhelming love for the creature. He took the roll from her mouth and caressed her head tenderly, saying with amazement, "Even when I'm not around, you're are still looking after me."

The dog jumped up, licking his hands in joyful adoration.

Wallace confessed, "I am going to miss *Mudryy*. She is a very special animal."

Rytsar looked at the pup with a new level of respect. "I agree. She is a very special girl."

Brie knelt down on the floor to pet her. She stared into the pup's eyes for a moment and asked, "You ever notice that some animals seem to have old souls?"

"*Mudryy* is definitely an old soul," Wallace agreed.

"I get that same feeling with Shadow," Brie told him, smiling.

Rytsar joined Brie down on the floor and the dog immediately switched her attention back to him. He looked deep into the animal's eyes and felt a quickening in his spirit.

"I've been calling her by the wrong name."

Wallace chuckled. "What do you mean?"

"Her name isn't *Mudryy* at all."

"What is it, then?"

He cupped her furry little head in both hands, smiling as tears of emotion ran down his face.

The animal's sweet spirit reminded him so much of Tatianna.

"Her name is *Vorobyshek.*"

My little sparrow…

Thank you so much for reading. I hope you enjoyed the 15th book in the Brie's Submission series.
The journey continues in ***In Sir's Arms***.

COMING NEXT

In Sir's Arms: Brie's Submission

16th Book in the Series

Available Now

Reviews mean the world to me!

I truly appreciate you taking the time to review
Her Russian Returns.

If you could leave a review on both Goodreads and the site where you purchased this book from, I would be so grateful. Sincerely, ~Red

If you are looking for more of Rytsar, my upcoming release *The Russian Unleashed* in July 2020 features Rytsar

The Russian Unleashed

Rytsar Durov – Fine vodka with a side of sadism.

Young, rich, and in charge, Rytsar is ready to take on the world.

Although his heart has been wounded, it still beats with a passion that can't be contained.

Click here to grab the book!

ABOUT THE AUTHOR

Over Two Million readers have enjoyed Red's stories

Red Phoenix – USA Today Bestselling Author

Winner of 8 Readers' Choice Awards

Hey Everyone!

I'm Red Phoenix, an author who also happens to be a submissive in real life. I wrote the Brie's Submission series because I wanted people everywhere to know just how much fun BDSM can be.

There is a huge cast of characters who are part of Brie's journey. The further you read into the story the more you learn about each one. I hope you grow to love Brie and the gang as much as I do.

They've become like family.

When I'm not writing, you can find me online with readers.

I heart my fans! ~Red

To find out more visit my Website

redphoenixauthor.com

Follow Me on BookBub

bookbub.com/authors/red-phoenix

Newsletter: Sign up

redphoenixauthor.com/newsletter-signup

Facebook: AuthorRedPhoenix

Twitter: @redphoenix69

Instagram: RedPhoenixAuthor

I invite you to join my reader Group!

facebook.com/groups/539875076052037

SIGN UP FOR MY NEWSLETTER HERE FOR THE LATEST RED PHOENIX UPDATES

FOLLOW ME ON INSTAGRAM

INSTAGRAM.COM/REDPHOENIXAUTHOR

SALES, GIVEAWAYS, NEW RELEASES, PREORDER LINKS, AND MORE!

SIGN UP HERE

REDPHOENIXAUTHOR.COM/NEWSLETTER-SIGNUP

Red Phoenix is the author of:

Brie's Submission Series:
Teach Me #1
Love Me #2
Catch Me #3
Try Me #4
Protect Me #5
Hold Me #6
Surprise Me #7
Trust Me #8
Claim Me #9
Enchant Me #10
A Cowboy's Heart #11
Breathe with Me #12
Her Russian Knight #13
Under His Protection #14
Her Russian Returns #15
In Sir's Arms #16
Bound by Love #17
Tied to Hope #18
Hope's First Christmas #19
Secrets of the Heart #20

***You can also purchase the** AUDIO BOOK **Versions**

Also part of the Submissive Training Center world:

Rise of the Dominates Trilogy
Sir's Rise #1
Master's Fate #2
The Russian Reborn #3

Captain's Duet
Safe Haven #1
Destined to Dominate #2

The Russian Unleashed #1

Other Books by Red Phoenix

Blissfully Undone

* Available in eBook and paperback

(Snowy Fun—Two people find themselves snowbound in a cabin where hidden love can flourish, taking one couple on a sensual journey into ménage à trois)

His Scottish Pet: Dom of the Ages

* Available in eBook and paperback

Audio Book: *His Scottish Pet: Dom of the Ages*

(Scottish Dom—A sexy Dom escapes to Scotland in the late 1400s. He encounters a waif who has the potential to free him from his tragic curse)

The Erotic Love Story of Amy and Troy

* Available in eBook and paperback

(Sexual Adventures—True love reigns, but fate continually throws Troy and Amy into the arms of others)

eBooks

Varick: The Reckoning

(Savory Vampire—A dark, sexy vampire story. The hero navigates the dangerous world he has been thrust into with lusty passion and a pure heart)

Keeper of the Wolf Clan (Keeper of Wolves, #1)

(Sexual Secrets—A virginal werewolf must act as the clan's mysterious Keeper)

The Keeper Finds Her Mate (Keeper of Wolves, #2)

(Second Chances—A young she-wolf must choose between old ties or new beginnings)

The Keeper Unites the Alphas (Keeper of Wolves, #3)

(Serious Consequences—The young she-wolf is captured by the rival clan)

Boxed Set: Keeper of Wolves Series (Books 1-3)

(Surprising Secrets—A secret so shocking it will rock Layla's world. The young she-wolf is put in a position of being able to save her werewolf clan or becoming the reason for its destruction)

Socrates Inspires Cherry to Blossom

(Satisfying Surrender—A mature and curvaceous woman becomes fascinated by an online Dom who has much to teach her)

By the Light of the Scottish Moon

(Saving Love—Two lost souls, the Moon, a werewolf, and a death wish…)

In 9 Days

(Sweet Romance—A young girl falls in love with the new student, nicknamed "the Freak")

---

9 Days and Counting

(Sacrificial Love—The sequel to *In 9 Days* delves into the emotional reunion of two longtime lovers)

And Then He Saved Me

(Saving Tenderness—When a young girl tries to kill herself, a man of great character intervenes with a love that heals)

Connect with Red on Substance B

Substance B is a platform for independent authors to directly connect with their readers. Please visit Red's Substance B page where you can:

- Sign up for Red's newsletter
- Send a message to Red
- See all platforms where Red's books are sold

Visit Substance B today to learn more about your favorite independent authors.

Made in USA - Kendallville, IN
1169177_9780692941584
09.23.2020 0905